Austin Dobson

Vignettes in Rhyme

and other verses

Austin Dobson

Vignettes in Rhyme
and other verses

ISBN/EAN: 9783337387266

Printed in Europe, USA, Canada, Australia, Japan

Cover: Foto ©Andreas Hilbeck / pixelio.de

More available books at **www.hansebooks.com**

VIGNETTES IN RHYME

AND OTHER VERSES

BY

AUSTIN DOBSON

" Majores majora sonent."

NEW YORK
HENRY HOLT AND COMPANY
1880

[*The verses in this volume are selected by the Author for this edition, and, with some few exceptions, are from* VIGNETTES IN RHYME, 1873, *and* PROVERBS IN PORCELAIN, 1877.]

INTRODUCTION.

An usher at the drawing-room door serves as a foil to the courtly groups beyond him. All his bows and flourishes seem commonplace beside the easy grace of his betters, if, indeed, the guests vouchsafe him a glance as they pass within. Little they care whether his legs be cross-gartered. Still, the usher is thought to be, in his way, a useful personage. And an introduction to these Vignettes in Rhyme thus may bear a certain fitness,—lest otherwise the collection should lack that effect which some prosaic contrast may lend to the delicate art of the whole.

Once acquainted with these pages, the reader will find that my comparison is an apt one; that he is in good company, and that Mr. Dobson, more than other recent poets, seems not only to gather about him a select concourse of fine people, but to move at ease among them. It is a pleasure to meet these gentlefolk, and like a mark of our own rank. Here are gathered, it is true, those of various periods and manners, but all demean themselves with graceful breeding and without affectation, and are on good terms with one another

v

and with their host. Here are the old noblesse, the *beau sabreur*, the gentleman and gentlewoman of the old school, and here the youths and maidens of to-day, —a choice assemblage, with not a prig, a bore, or a vulgarian among them.

Some of the most attractive portions of this selection, therefore, have to do with the quaint people of a time gone by, and with the treasures they have bequeathed to us. But the author is an artist of the present, and his work a product of to-day. Its modernism is a constant charm. There are in England and France so many lovely relics of a refined, alluring age! In England, the canvases of Sir Joshua and Gainsborough, the old houses with their souvenirs of teacup-times,— brocade and chintz, deftly garnished mantels, tapestried and lavendered chambers, box-bordered lawns and garden-plots. In France, the dark hangings and polished floors of stately mirrored rooms in turreted châteaux and peaked mansions. Never so much as now have the artists availed themselves of these materials, and of the riches of galleries and museums close at hand. But one looks to the poet to catch the sense and soul of these things, the aroma that clings about them. The fashions that most readily appeal to Mr. Dobson are those which are so far by-gone as to be again desired and new. What more odious than the mode we have just discarded? What so winning as that of a time earlier than our memory, and thoroughly good in its time? The movement which has given expression to all this, on both sides of the ocean, is like a new taste. Mr. Dobson is the instinctive and born interpreter of its sentiment, and his Vignettes in Rhyme will be as welcome to us as they have been to his own people. The actor's art delights us, because we know it is not real, and the modern renaissance delights us, because it gives us something quite apart from our common humdrum life; it is a feeling of to-day that dallies with the fragments of the past,—of that Past which never is past, which merges with the Present, and retains a hold upon our works of everyday use and beauty.

I write first of Mr. Dobson's old-time sentiment, because it is so definite and effective, but his muse is not restricted to a single range. Before looking farther, let us see who is this artist that has filled the vacant niche, and whose verse shows at once the strength and fineness that make it rank with the selectest poetry of our day.

Not unlike others who live at will in an ideal world, Austin Dobson is as modest and unassuming a person as one often meets. Just a poet, scholar and gentleman, the artist-side of whose nature compensates him for any lack of adventure in his daily work and walk. As is the case with many London authors, an office in the Civil Service has supplied him with an honorable certainty of livelihood and left his heart at ease for song. He was born in 1840, and has been a government-clerk for twenty-two years. Singularly enough, he did not begin to write poetry till he was twenty-five years of age, and the first collection of his "Vignettes" was not made until 1874. From the outset he took the public taste with the delicate sense and humor of his lyrics, no less than by their finish and ideality. We reasonably may surmise that years of growth, study, observation, lay behind this good fortune.

My own attention, I remember, first was drawn to his work by the neatest and brightest of society-verse, composed in a novel style, quite unlike that of Praed, Locker, or his earlier predecessors. I have elsewhere described poems of this class as "those patrician rhymes, which, for want of an English equivalent, are termed *vers de société.* . . . This is pervaded by an indefinable grace that elevates it to the region of poetic art, and owing to which the lightest ballads of Suckling and Waller are current to this day. In fine, the true kind is marked by humor, by spontaneity, joined with extreme elegance of finish, by the quality we call breeding,—above all, by lightness of touch." All of these essentials were present in "Tu Quoque," "An Autumn Idyll," and in other pieces which at once brought Mr. Dobson into favor. Some of them are so witty and elegant, surrounded by so fine an atmosphere, and withal so true to the feeling and scenery of his own island, as to make him seem like a modern Horace or Theocritus, or like both in one. He is not the first poet that has been called an English Horace, but few have better merited the title. He draws his Englishmen as Horace drew his town and country friends. It seems to me that he is the sketcher to whom Thackeray would take a liking. Since the De Floracs, we have had no such

French people as L'Étoile and Monsieur Vieuxbois; since Esmond and his times, no such people of the old England have come to life again as Mr. Dobson's "Gentleman" and "Gentlewoman," his "Dorothy," or even that knight of the road, whose untimely taking-off is rehearsed in "The Ballad of 'Beau Brocade'."

Our debonair poet elevates taste and feeling to the pitch of imagination. He yields himself to the spell of brooding memories and associations:

> "We shut our hearts up, now-a-days,
> Like some old music-box that plays
> Unfashionable airs that raise
>   Derisive pity;
> Alas,—a nothing starts the spring:
> And lo, the sentimental thing
> At once commences, quavering
>   Its lover's ditty.

His pathos and tenderness appear, too, in more serious pieces. There are kind touches in "The Child-Musician," "The Cradle," and "A Nightingale in Kensington Gardens." Mr. Brander Matthews, one of our own most agreeable writers, justly lays stress upon Dobson's perfect absorption in his immediate theme, his art of shutting out from a poem everything foreign to its needs. How purely Greek the image of Autonoë! How minute the picture of "An Old Fish-Pond," and what shrewd wisdom! What human nature in "A Dead Letter," one of my favorite pieces,—and how perfect its reproduction of the ancestral mode! With all his regard for "values," the poet never goes to the pseudo-æsthetic extreme; indeed, he is the first to poke fun at it, and seems quite free from certain affectations of modern verse. His English is pure and simple, and the natural finish of his poetry shows for itself. I doubt if there is another collection of lyrics by an English singer more devoid of blemishes, more difficult to amend by the striking-out or change of words and measures. Mr. Aldrich has suggested that it may well be compared, in this respect, to the French of such an artist as Théophile Gautier,—the lesson of whose L'Art, as will be seen from his own crystalline poem in imitation, Mr. Dobson long ago took to heart.

His lyrical studies and dialogues upon French themes of the Eighteenth Century are full of poetic realism. In "Une Marquise," and in "The Story of Rosina,"—a sustained piece which shows the higher range of its author's genius,—the presiding beauty, and the artist of a time and a region

"Wherein most things went naked, save the Truth,"

are made known to us more truly than they dared to know themselves. For dainty workmanship, and comprehension of the spirit of an age, read "The Metamorphosis," and its sequel "The Song out of Season." What other poet could have written these, or "Goodnight, Babette!"—which contains the Angelus song, whose loveliness I scarcely realized until Mr. Aldrich printed it by itself, a gem taken from its setting. And I know not, since reading "The Curé's Progress," where else to find so attractive an ideal of the goodness, quaintness, sweetness, of the typical *Père* on his journey down the street of his little town. The town itself is depicted, in a few stanzas, as plainly as "Our Village" in the whole series of Miss Mitford's classic sketches.

Mr. Dobson escapes the restrictions of many writers of elegant verse by his refreshing variety. In his lightest work he is a fine poet at play; not a weakling, with one pretty gift, doing the best thing in his power. He is entitled to the credit, whatever that may be, of having been among the first to really bring into fashion the present use of old French stanzaic and rhythmic forms. In view of the speed wherewith these have been adopted and played upon by poets and parodists without number, I am not sure whether to thank him or to condole with him. We must acknowledge that English poetry, like the language, is eclectic, deriving its richness from many sources. Its lyrical score, which long has been too monotonous, doubtless will gain something from the revival of these continental forms. Only those suited to the genius of our song will come into permanent use. If any readers are as yet unacquainted with the nature and varieties of these old-new forms, they can find the best exposition of them in Mr. Edmund Gosse's "Plea for Certain Exotic Forms of Verse."[1] The specimens of the Rondel, the Rondeau, the Triolet, the Villanelle, the Ballade, the Chant Royal, which he cites from the works of Swin-

---

[1] *Cornhill Magazine,* July, 1877.

burne, Lang, Dobson, and those of his own sweet and learned muse, are excellently done. Nearer home, we have Mr. Matthews's analysis[1] of Mr. Dobson's experiments in all these forms of verse, and a farther description on my part is rendered unnecessary.

Most of the poems of this class in the following pages first were brought together systematically in Dobson's "Proverbs in Porcelain," 1877, although all of their modes, except the Chant Royal and the Villanelle, can be found in the relics of early English poetry, —some even in the verse of Gower and Chaucer. My own creed is that the chief question is not what novelty tempts us to the show, but whether the show be a good one,—and Mr. Dobson pleasantly avows a kindred belief. Some of these exotic forms seem to be handled as cleverly by him in English, as in French by De Banville. The *villanelle* "For a Copy of Theocritus," is like a necklace of beaten antique gold. His *rondeaux* "To Ethel" and "When *Finis* Comes," have a tricksy spirit, a winged and subtle perfection. Their rules seem peculiarly suited to experiments in translation from Horace. At all events, I do not recall any paraphrases of "O Fons Bandusiæ" and "Vixi Puellis" more satisfactory in form and flavor than those which Mr. Dobson gives us.

Reviewing these "Vignettes in Rhyme" and "Proverbs in Porcelain," I have felt like one who has the freedom of a virtuoso's collection,—who handles unique

---

[1] *Appleton's Journal,* June, 1878.

and precious things, fearing that his clumsiness may leave a blemish or in some way cost him dear. Artist and poet at once, Mr. Dobson reminds me of Francia, who "loved to sign his paintings 'Aurifex,' and on his trinkets inscribed the word 'Pictor'," and I have an impression that rarely of late has an English singer offered us more charming portraits, purer touches of nature, more picturesque glimpses of a manor which he holds in fee. It is hard to define his limitations, for he has not yet gone beyond them; yet I shall not be surprised if his future career shall prove them to be outside the "liberties" which even a friendly critic might assign to him.

EDMUND C. STEDMAN.

NEW YORK, *January*, 1880.

xiii

To you I sing, whom towns immure,
And bonds of toil hold fast and sure ;—
   To you across whose aching sight
   Come woodlands bathed in April light,
And dreams of pastime premature.

And you, O Sad, who still endure
Some wound that only Time can cure,—
   To you, in watches of the night,
         To you I sing !

But most to you with eyelids pure,
Scarce witting yet of love or lure ;—
   To you, with bird-like glances bright,
Half-paused to speak, half-poised in flight ;—
O English Girl, divine, demure,
         To YOU *I sing !*

CONTENTS.

xv

Contents.

Contents.

Contents.

VIGNETTES IN RHYME.

THE DRAMA OF THE DOCTOR'S WINDOW.

IN THREE ACTS, WITH A PROLOGUE.

" A tedious brief scene of young Pyramus,
And his love Thisbe; very tragical mirth."
—MIDSUMMER-NIGHT'S DREAM.

PROLOGUE.

"WELL, I must wait!"   The Doctor's room,
　　Where I used this expression,
　Wore the severe official gloom
　　Attached to that profession;
　Rendered severer by a bald
　　And skinless Gladiator,
　Whose raw robustness first appalled
　　The entering spectator.

The Drama of the Doctor's Window.

No one would call "The Lancet" gay,—
  Few could avoid confessing
That Jones "On Muscular Decay"
  Is, as a rule, depressing:
So, leaving both, to change the scene,
  I turned toward the shutter,
And peered out vacantly between
  A water-butt and gutter.

Below, the Doctor's garden lay,
  If thus imagination
May dignify a square of clay
  Unused to vegetation,
Filled with a dismal-looking swing—
  That brought to mind a gallows—
An empty kennel, mouldering,
  And two dyspeptic aloes.

No sparrow chirped, no daisy sprung,
  About the place deserted;
Only across the swing-board hung
  A battered doll, inverted,
Which sadly seemed to disconcert
  The vagrant cat that scanned it,
Sniffed doubtfully around the skirt,
  But failed to understand it.

2

A dreary spot!   And yet, I own,
　　Half hoping that, perchance, it
Might, in some unknown way, atone
　　For Jones and for "The Lancet,"
I watched; and by especial grace,
　　Within this stage contracted,
Saw presently before my face
　　A classic story acted.

Ah, World of ours, are you so gray
　　And weary, World, of spinning,
That you repeat the tales to-day
　　You told at the beginning?
For lo! the same old myths that made
　　The early "stage successes,"
Still "hold the boards," and still are played,
　　"With new effects and dresses."

Small, lonely, "three-pair-backs" behold,
　　To-day, Alcestis dying;
To-day, in farthest Polar cold,
　　Ulysses' bones are lying;
Still in one's morning "Times" one reads
　　How fell an Indian Hector;
Still clubs discuss Achilles' steeds,
　　Briseis' next protector;—

3

Still Menelaus brings, we see,
　　His oft-remanded case on;
Still somewhere sad Hypsipyle
　　Bewails a faithless Jason;
And here, the Doctor's sill beside,
　　Do I not now discover
A Thisbe, whom the walls divide
　　From Pyramus, her lover?

ACT THE FIRST.

Act I. began.　Some noise had scared
　　The cat, that like an arrow
Shot up the wall and disappeared;
　　And then across the narrow,
Unweeded path, a small dark thing,
　　Hid by a garden-bonnet,
Passed wearily towards the swing,
　　Paused, turned, and climbed upon it.

A child of five, with eyes that were
　　At least a decade older,
A mournful mouth, and tangled hair
　　Flung careless round her shoulder,
Dressed in a stiff ill-fitting frock,
　　Whose black uncomely rigour

Seemed to sardonically mock
  The plaintive, slender figure.

What was it?   Something in the dress
  That told the girl unmothered;
Or was it that the merciless
  Black garb of mourning smothered
Life and all light :—but rocking so,
  In the dull garden-corner,
The lonely swinger seemed to grow
  More piteous and forlorner.

Then, as I looked, across the wall
  Of " next-door's " garden, that is—
To speak correctly—through its tall
  Surmounting fence of lattice,
Peeped a boy's face, with curling hair,
  Ripe lips, half drawn asunder,
And round, bright eyes, that wore a stare
  Of frankest childish wonder.

Rounder they grew by slow degrees,
  Until the swinger, swerving,
Made, all at once, alive to these
  Intentest orbs observing,

Gave just one brief, half-uttered cry,
  And,—as with gathered kirtle,
Nymphs fly from Pan's head suddenly
  Thrust through the budding myrtle,—

Fled in dismay.   A moment's space,
  The eyes looked almost tragic;
Then, when they caught my watching face,
  Vanished as if by magic;
And, like some sombre thing beguiled
  To strange, unwonted laughter,
The gloomy garden having smiled,
  Became the gloomier after.

ACT THE SECOND.

Yes: they were gone, the stage was bare,—
  Blank as before; and therefore,
Sinking within the patient's chair,
  Half vexed, I knew not wherefore,
I dozed; till, startled by some call,
  A glance sufficed to show me,
The boy again above the wall,
  The girl erect below me.

The boy, it seemed, to add a force
  To words found unavailing,

6

Had pushed a striped and spotted horse
    Half through the blistered paling,
Where now it stuck, stiff-legged and straight,
    While he, in exultation,
Chattered some half-articulate
    Excited explanation.

Meanwhile, the girl, with upturned face,
    Stood motionless, and listened;
The ill-cut frock had gained a grace,
    The pale hair almost glistened;
The figure looked alert and bright,
    Buoyant as though some power
Had lifted it, as rain at night
    Uplifts a drooping flower.

The eyes had lost their listless way,—
    The old life, tired and faded,
Had slipped down with the doll that lay
    Before her feet, degraded;
She only, yearning upward, found
    In those bright eyes above her
The ghost of some enchanted ground
    Where even Nurse would love her.

Ah, tyrant Time! you hold the book,
    We, sick and sad, begin it;

You close it fast, if we but look
    Pleased for a meagre minute;
You closed it now, for, out of sight,
    Some warning finger beckoned;
Exeunt both to left and right;—
    Thus ended Act the Second.

ACT THE THIRD.

Or so it proved.   For while I still
    Believed them gone for ever,
Half raised above the window sill,
    I saw the lattice quiver;
And lo, once more appeared the head,
    Flushed, while the round mouth pouted;
" Give Tom a kiss," the red lips said,
    In style the most undoubted.

The girl came back without a thought;
    Dear Muse of Mayfair, pardon,
If more restraint had not been taught
    In this neglected garden;
For these your code was all too stiff,
    So, seeing none dissented,
Their unfeigned faces met as if
    Manners were not invented.

8

Then on the scene,—by happy fate,
　　When lip from lip had parted,
And, therefore, just two seconds late,—
　　A sharp-faced nurse-maid darted;
Swooped on the boy, as swoops a kite
　　Upon a rover chicken,
And bore him sourly off, despite
　　His well-directed kicking.

The girl stood silent, with a look
　　Too subtle to unravel,
Then, with a sudden gesture took
　　The torn doll from the gravel;
Hid the whole face, with one caress,
　　Under the garden-bonnet,
And, passing in, I saw her press
　　Kiss after kiss upon it.

Exeunt omnes.　End of play.
　　It made the dull room brighter,
The Gladiator almost gay,
　　And e'en "The Lancet" lighter.

9

AN AUTUMN IDYLL.

" Sweet Themmes! runne softly, till I end my song."
—SPENSER.

LAWRENCE.   FRANK.   JACK.

LAWRENCE.

HERE, where the beech-nuts drop among the grasses,
   Push the boat in, and throw the rope ashore.
Jack, hand me out the claret and the glasses;
   Here let us sit.   We landed here before.

FRANK.

Jack 's undecided.   Say, *formose puer*,
   Bent in a dream above the "water wan,"
Shall we row higher, for the reeds are fewer,
   There by the pollards, where you see the swan?

10

An Autumn Idyll.

JACK.

Hist! That 's a pike. Look—nose against the river,
　Gaunt as a wolf,—the sly old privateer!
Enter a gudgeon. Snap,—a gulp, a shiver;—
　Exit the gudgeon. Let us anchor here.

FRANK (*in the grass*).

Jove, what a day! Black Care upon the crupper
　Nods at his post, and slumbers in the sun;
Half of Theocritus, with a touch of Tupper,
　Churns in my head. The frenzy has begun!

LAWRENCE.

Sing to us then. Damœtas in a choker,
　Much out of tune, will edify the rooks.

FRANK.

Sing you again. So musical a croaker
　Surely will draw the fish upon the hooks.

JACK.

Sing while you may. The beard of manhood still is
　Faint on your cheeks, but I, alas! am old.
Doubtless you yet believe in Amaryllis;—
　Sing me of Her, whose name may not be told.

An Autumn Idyll.

FRANK.

Listen, O Thames! His budding beard is riper,
    Say—by a week. Well, Lawrence, shall we sing?

LAWRENCE.

Yes, if you will. But ere I play the piper,
    Let him declare the prize he has to bring.

JACK.

Hear then, my Shepherds. Lo, to him accounted
    First in the song, a Pipe I will impart;—
This, my Belovèd, marvellously mounted,
    Amber and foam,—a miracle of art.

LAWRENCE.

Lordly the gift. O Muse of many numbers,
    Grant me a soft alliterative song!

FRANK.

Me too, O Muse! And when the Umpire slumbers
    Sting him with gnats a summer evening long.

LAWRENCE.

Not in a cot, begarlanded of spiders,
    Not where the brook traditionally "purls,"—
No, in the Row, supreme among the riders,
    Seek I the gem,—the paragon of girls.

FRANK.

Not in the waste of column and of coping,
    Not in the sham and stucco of a square,—
No, on a June-lawn, to the water sloping,
    Stands she I honour, beautifully fair.

LAWRENCE.

Dark-haired is mine, with splendid tresses plaited
    Back from the brows, imperially curled;
Calm as a grand, far-looking Caryatid,
    Holding the roof that covers in a world.

FRANK.

Dark-haired is mine, with breezy ripples swinging
    Loose as a vine-branch blowing in the morn;
Eyes like the morning, mouth for ever singing,
    Blithe as a bird new risen from the corn.

LAWRENCE.

Best is the song with music interwoven:
    Mine 's a musician,—musical at heart,—
Throbs to the gathered grieving of Beethoven,
    Sways to the light coquetting of Mozart.

FRANK.

Best? You should hear mine trilling out a ballad,
    Queen at a pic-nic, leader of the glees,

Not too divine to toss you up a salad,
   Great in Sir Roger danced among the trees.

LAWRENCE.

Ah, when the thick night flares with drooping torches,
   Ah, when the crush-room empties of the swarm,
Pleasant the hand that, in the gusty porches,
   Light as a snow-flake, settles on your arm.

FRANK.

Better the twilight and the cheery chatting,—
   Better the dim, forgotten garden-seat,
Where one may lie, and watch the fingers tatting,
   Lounging with Bran or Bevis at her feet.

LAWRENCE.

All worship mine.   Her purity doth hedge her
   Round with so delicate divinity, that men,
Stained to the soul with money-bag and ledger,
   Bend to the goddess, manifest again.

FRANK.

None worship mine.   But some, I fancy, love her,—
   Cynics to boot.   I know the children run,
Seeing her come, for naught that I discover,
   Save that she brings the summer and the sun.

14

An Autumn Idyll.

LAWRENCE.

Mine is a Lady, beautiful and queenly,
  Crowned with a sweet, continual control,
Grandly forbearing, lifting life serenely
  E'en to her own nobility of soul.

FRANK.

Mine is a Woman, kindly beyond measure,
  Fearless in praising, faltering in blame;
Simply devoted to other people's pleasure,—
  Jack's sister Florence,—now you know her name.

LAWRENCE.

"Jack's sister Florence!" Never, Francis, never.
  Jack, do you hear? Why, it was she I meant.
She like the country! Ah, she's far too clever—

FRANK.

There you are wrong. I know her down in Kent.

LAWRENCE.

You'll get a sunstroke, standing with your head bare.
Sorry to differ. Jack,—the word's with you.

FRANK.

How is it, Umpire? Though the motto's thread-
    bare,
  "*Cælum, non animum*"—is, I take it, true.

JACK.

" *Souvent femme varie,*" as a rule, is truer;
    Flattered, I 'm sure,—but both of you romance.
  Happy to further suit of either wooer,
    Merely observing—you have n't got a chance.

LAWRENCE.

Yes.   But the Pipe—

FRANK.

                    The Pipe is what we care for,—

JACK.

  Well, in this case, I scarcely need explain,
  Judgment of mine were indiscreet, and therefore,—
    Peace to you both.   The Pipe I shall retain.

16

A GARDEN IDYLL.

A LADY.   **A POET.**

The Lady.

Sir Poet, ere you crossed the lawn
   (If it was wrong to watch you, pardon,)
Behind this weeping birch withdrawn,
   I watched you saunter round the garden.
I saw you bend beside the phlox,
   Pluck, as you passed, a sprig of myrtle,
Review my well-ranged hollyhocks,
   Smile at the fountain's slender spurtle;

You paused beneath the cherry-tree,
   Where my marauder thrush was singing,
Peered at the bee-hives curiously,
   And narrowly escaped a stinging;

And then—you see I watched—you passed
   Down the espalier walk that reaches
Out to the western wall, and last
   Dropped on the seat before the peaches.

What was your thought? You waited long.
   Sublime or graceful,—grave,—satiric?
A Morris Greek-and-Gothic song?
   A tender Tennysonian lyric?
Tell me. That garden-seat shall be,
   So long as speech renown disperses,
Illustrious as the spot where he—
   The gifted Blank—composed his verses.

THE POET.

Madam,—whose uncensorious eye
   Grows gracious over certain pages,
Wherein the Jester's maxims lie,
   It may be, thicker than the Sage's—
I hear but to obey, and could
   Mere wish of mine the pleasure do you,
Some verse as whimsical as Hood,—
   As gay as Praed,—should answer to you.

But, though the common voice proclaims
   Our only serious vocation

A Garden Idyll.

Confined to giving nothings names,
    And dreams a "local habitation";
Believe me there are tuneless days,
    When neither marble, brass, nor vellum,
Would profit much by any lays
    That haunt the poet's cerebellum.

More empty things, I fear, than rhymes,
    More idle things than songs, absorb it;
The "finely-frenzied" eye, at times,
    Reposes mildly in its orbit;
And—painful truth—at times, to him,
    Whose jog-trot thought is nowise restive,
"A primrose by a river's brim"
    Is absolutely unsuggestive.

The fickle Muse! As ladies will,
    She sometimes wearies of her wooer;
A goddess, yet a woman still,
    She flies the more that we pursue her;
In short, with worst as well as best,
    Five months in six, your hapless poet
Is just as prosy as the rest,
    But cannot comfortably show it.

You thought, no doubt, the garden-scent
    Brings back some brief-winged bright sensation

A Garden Idyll.

Of love that came and love that went,—
    Some fragrance of a lost flirtation,
Born when the cuckoo changes song,
    Dead ere the apple's red is on it,
That should have been an epic long,
    Yet scarcely served to fill a sonnet.

Or else you thought,—the murmuring noon,
    He turns it to a lyric sweeter,
With birds that gossip in the tune,
    And windy bough-swing in the metre;
Or else the zigzag fruit-tree arms
    Recall some dream of harp-prest bosoms,
Round singing mouths, and chanted charms,
    And mediæval orchard blossoms,—

Quite *à la mode.* Alas for prose,—
    My vagrant fancies only rambled
Back to the red-walled Rectory close,
    Where first my graceless boyhood gamboled,
Climbed on the dial, teased the fish,
    And chased the kitten round the beeches,
Till widening instincts made me wish
    For certain slowly-ripening peaches.

Three peaches.   Not the Graces three
    Had more equality of beauty:

A Garden Idyll.

I would not look, yet went to see;
   I wrestled with Desire and Duty;
I felt the pangs of those who feel
   The Laws of Property beset them;
The conflict made my reason reel,
   And, half-abstractedly, I ate them ;—

Or Two of them.   Forthwith Despair—
   More keen that one of these was rotten—
Moved me to seek some forest lair
   Where I might hide and dwell forgotten,
Attired in skins, by berries stained,
   Absolved from brushes and ablution ;—
But, ere my sylvan haunt was gained,
   Fate gave me up to execution.

I saw it all but now.   The grin
   That gnarled old Gardener Sandy's features,
My father, scholar-like and thin,
   Unroused, the tenderest of creatures;
I saw—ah me—I saw again
   My dear and deprecating mother;
And then, remembering the cane,
   Regretted—that *I'd left the other.*

TU QUOQUE.

AN IDYLL IN THE CONSERVATORY.

" —romprons-nous,
Ou ne romprons-nous pas ? "
—Le Dépit Amoureux.

NELLIE.

If I were you, when ladies at the play, sir,
  Beckon and nod, a melodrama through,
I would not turn abstractedly away, sir,
    If I were you!

FRANK.

If I were you, when persons I affected,
  Wait for three hours to take me down to Kew,
I would, at least, pretend I recollected,
    If I were you!

22

Tu Quoque.

NELLIE.

If I were you, when ladies are so lavish,
   Sir, as to keep me every waltz but two,
I would not dance with *odious* Miss M'Tavish,
   If I were you!

FRANK.

If I were you, who vow you cannot suffer
   Whiff of the best,—the mildest "honey-dew,"
I would not dance with smoke-consuming Puffer,
   If I were you!

NELLIE.

If I were you, I would not, sir, be bitter,
   Even to write the "Cynical Review";—

FRANK.

No, I should doubtless find flirtation fitter,
   If I were you!

NELLIE.

Really! You would? Why, Frank, you 're quite
     delightful,—
   Hot as Othello, and as black of hue;
Borrow my fan. I would not look so *frightful*,
   If I were you!

Tu Quoque.

FRANK.

" It is the cause." I mean your chaperon is
    Bringing some well-curled juvenile. Adieu!
I shall retire. I 'd spare that poor Adonis,
    If I were you!

NELLIE.

Go, if you will. At once! And by express, sir!
    Where shall it be? To China—or Peru?
Go. I should leave inquirers my address, sir,
    If I were you!

FRANK.

No,—I remain. To stay and fight a duel
    Seems, on the whole, the proper thing to do—
Ah, you are strong,—I would not then be cruel,
    If I were you!

NELLIE.

One does not like one's feelings to be doubted,—

FRANK.

One does not like one's friends to misconstrue,—

NELLIE.

If I confess that I a wee-bit pouted?—

24

FRANK.

I should admit that I was *piqué,* too.

NELLIE.

Ask me to dance. I 'd say no more about it,
  If I were you!

[Waltz—*Exeunt.*]

A DIALOGUE FROM PLATO.

" Le temps le mieux employé est celui qu'on perd."
—CLAUDE TILLIER.

I 'D "read" three hours.   Both notes and text
   Were fast a mist becoming;
In bounced a vagrant bee, perplexed,
   And filled the room with humming,

Then out.   The casement's leafage sways,
   And, parted light, discloses
Miss Di., with hat and book,—a maze
   Of muslin mixed with roses.

"You 're reading Greek?"   "I am—and you?"
   "O, mine 's a mere romancer!"
"So Plato is."   "Then read him—do;
   And I 'll read mine in answer."

26

I read. "My Plato (Plato, too,—
    That wisdom thus should harden!)
Declares 'blue eyes look doubly blue
    Beneath a Dolly Varden.'"

She smiled. "My book in turn avers
    (No author's name is stated)
That sometimes those Philosophers
    Are sadly mis-translated."

" But hear,—the next 's in stronger style:
    The Cynic School asserted
That two red lips which part and smile
    May not be controverted!"

She smiled once more—"My book, I find,
    Observes some modern doctors
Would make the Cynics out a kind
    Of album-verse concoctors."

Then I—"Why not? 'Ephesian law,
    No less than time's tradition,
Enjoined fair speech on all who saw
    DIANA's apparition.'"

She blushed—this time. "If Plato's page
    No wiser precept teaches,

A Dialogue from Plato.

Then I 'd renounce that doubtful sage,
  And walk to Burnham-beeches."

" Agreed," I said. " For Socrates
  (I find he too is talking)
Thinks Learning can't remain at ease
  While Beauty goes a-walking."

She read no more. I leapt the sill:
  The sequel 's scarce essential—
Nay, more than this, I hold it still
  Profoundly confidential.

THE ROMAUNT OF THE ROSE.

Poor Rose!   I lift you from the street—
  Far better I should own you
Than you should lie for random feet
  Where careless hands have thrown you.

Poor pinky petals, crushed and torn!
  Did heartless Mayfair use you,
Then cast you forth to lie forlorn,
  For chariot wheels to bruise you?

I saw you last in Edith's hair.
  Rose, you would scarce discover
That I she passed upon the stair
  Was Edith's favoured lover,

A month—"a little month"—ago—
  O theme for moral writer!—

'Twixt you and me, my Rose, you know,
    She might have been politer;

But let that pass.   She gave you then—
    Behind the oleander—
To one, perhaps, of all the men,
    Who best could understand her,—

Cyril, that, duly flattered, took,
    As only Cyril 's able,
With just the same Arcadian look
    He used, last night, for Mabel;

Then, having waltzed till every star
    Had paled away in morning,
Lit up his cynical cigar,
    And tossed you downward, scorning.

Kismet, my Rose!   Revenge is sweet,—
    She made my heart-strings quiver;
And yet—You shan't lie in the street,
    I 'll drop you in the River.

LOVE IN WINTER.

Between the berried holly-bush
The Blackbird whistled to the Thrush:
"Which way did bright-eyed Bella go?
Look, Speckle-breast, across the snow,—
Are those her dainty tracks I see,
That wind toward the shrubbery?"

The Throstle pecked the berries still.
"No need for looking, Yellow-bill;
Young Frank was there an hour ago,
Half frozen, waiting in the snow;
His callow beard was white with rime,—
Tchuck,—'t is a merry pairing-time!"

"What would you?" twittered in the Wren;
"These are the reckless ways of men.

Love in Winter.

I watched them bill and coo as though
They thought the sign of Spring was snow;
If men but timed their loves as we,
'T would save this inconsistency."

" Nay, Gossip," chirped the Robin, "nay;
I like their unreflective way.
Besides, I heard enough to show
Their love is proof against the snow :—
Why wait,' he said, 'why wait for May,
When love can warm a winter's day?'"

POT-POURRI.

" Si jeunesse savait ?—"

I PLUNGE my hand among the leaves:
(An alien touch but dust perceives,
  Nought else supposes;)
For me those fragrant ruins raise
Clear memory of the vanished days
  When they were roses.

" If youth but knew!" Ah, "if," in truth—
I can recall with what gay youth,
  To what light chorus,
Unsobered yet by time or change,
We roamed the many-gabled Grange,
  All life before us;

33

Braved the old clock-tower's dust and damp
To catch the dim Arthurian camp
    In misty distance;
Peered at the still-room's sacred stores,
Or rapped at walls for sliding doors
    Of feigned existence.

What need had we for thoughts or cares!
The hot sun parched the old parterres
    And "flowerful closes";
We roused the rooks with rounds and glees,
Played hide-and-seek behind the trees,—
    Then plucked these roses.

Louise was one—light, glib Louise,
So freshly freed from school decrees
    You scarce could stop her;
And Bell, the Beauty, unsurprised
At fallen locks that scandalized
    Our dear " Miss Proper:"—

Shy Ruth, all heart and tenderness,
Who wept—like Chaucer's Prioress,
    When Dash was smitten;
Who blushed before the mildest men,
Yet waxed a very Corday when
    You teased her kitten.

I loved them all.   Bell first and best;
Louise the next—for days of jest
    Or madcap masking;
And Ruth, I thought,—why, failing these,
When my High-Mightiness should please,
    She 'd come for asking.

   .   .   .   .   .

Louise was grave when last we met;
Bell's beauty, like a sun, has set ;
    And Ruth, Heaven bless her,
Ruth that I wooed,—and wooed in vain,
Has gone where neither grief nor pain
   ·Can now distress her.

35

DOROTHY.

A RÊVERIE SUGGESTED BY THE NAME UPON A PANE.

SHE then must once have looked, as I
Look now, across the level rye,—
Past Church and Manor-house, and seen,
As now I see, the village green,
The bridge, and Walton's river—she
Whose old-world name was "Dorothy."

The swallows must have twittered, too,
Above her head; the roses blew
Below, no doubt,—and, sure, the South
Crept up the wall and kissed her mouth,—
That wistful mouth, which comes to me
Linked with her name of Dorothy.

36

Dorothy.

What was she like?   I picture her
Unmeet for uncouth worshipper;—
Soft,—pensive,—far too subtly graced
To suit the blunt bucolic taste,
Whose crude perception could but see
" Ma'am Fine-airs" in Miss Dorothy.

How not?   She loved, may be, perfume,
Soft textures, lace, a half-lit room;—
Perchance too candidly preferred
"Clarissa" to a gossip's word;—
And, for the rest, would seem to be
Or proud, or dull—this Dorothy.

Poor child, with heart the down-lined nest
Of warmest instincts unconfest,
Soft callow things that vaguely felt
The breeze caress, the sunlight melt,
But yet, by some obscure decree
Unwinged from birth;—poor Dorothy!

Not less I dream her mute desire
To acred churl and booby squire,
Now pale, with timorous eyes that filled
At "twice-told tales" of foxes killed;—
Now trembling when slow tongues grew free
'Twixt sport, and Port—and Dorothy!

'T was then she 'd seek this nook, and find
Its evening landscape balmy-kind;
And here, where still hér gentle name
Lives on the old green glass, would frame
Fond dreams of unfound harmony
'Twixt heart and heart.   Poor Dorothy!

L'ENVOI.

These last I spoke.   Then Florence said,
Below me,—"Dreams?   Delusions, Fred!"
Next, with a pause,—she bent the while
Over a rose, with roguish smile—
"But how disgusted, sir, you 'll be
To hear *I* scrawled that 'Dorothy.'"

38

AVICE.

" On serait tenté de lui dire, Bonjour, Mademoiselle la Bergeronnette."—VICTOR HUGO.

THOUGH the voice of modern schools
   Has demurred,
By the dreamy Asian creed
   'T is averred,
That the souls of men, released
From their bodies when deceased,
Sometimes enter in a beast,—
   Or a bird.

I have watched you long, Avice,—
   Watched you so,
I have found your secret out;
   And I know
That the restless ribboned things,
Where your slope of shoulder springs,
Are but undeveloped wings
   That will grow.

39

Avice.

When you enter in a room,
        It is stirred
With the wayward, flashing flight
        Of a bird;
And you speak—and bring with you
Leaf and sun-ray, bud and blue,
And the wind-breath and the dew
        At a word.

When you called to me my name,
        Then again
When I heard your single cry
        In the lane,
All the sound was as the "sweet"
Which the birds to birds repeat
In their thank-song to the heat
        After rain.

When you sang the *Schwalbenlied*,
        'T was absurd,—
But it seemed no human note
        That I heard;
For your strain had all the trills,
All the little shakes and stills,
Of the over-song that rills
        From a bird.

Avice.

You have just their eager, quick
$\qquad$ " *Airs de tête*,"
All their flush and fever-heat
$\qquad$ When elate;
Every bird-like nod and beck,
And a bird's own curve of neck
When she gives a little peck
$\qquad$ To her mate.

When you left me, only now,
$\qquad$ In that furred,
Puffed, and feathered Polish dress,
$\qquad$ I was spurred
Just to catch you, O my Sweet,
By the bodice trim and neat,—
Just to feel your heart a-beat,
$\qquad$ Like a bird.

Yet, alas!   Love's light you deign
$\qquad$ But to wear
As the dew upon your plumes,
$\qquad$ And you care
Not a whit for rest or hush;
But the leaves, the lyric gush,
And the wing-power, and the rush
$\qquad$ Of the air.

Avice.

So I dare not woo you, Sweet,
   For a day,
Lest I lose you in a flash,
   As I may;
Did I tell you tender things,
You would shake your sudden wings;—
You would start from him who sings,
   And away.

THE LOVE-LETTER.

" J'ai vu les mœurs de mon tems, et j'ai publié cette lettre."
—LA NOUVELLE HÉLOISE.

IF this should fail, why then I scarcely know
    What could succeed. Here 's brilliancy (and
        banter),
Byron *ad lib.*, a chapter of Rousseau ;—
    If this should fail, then *tempora mutantur ;*
Style 's out of date, and love, as a profession,
Acquires no aid from beauty of expression.

" The men who think as I, I fear, are few,"
    (Cynics would say 't were well if they were fewer)
" I am not what I seem,"—(indeed, 't is true ;
    Though, as a sentiment, it might be newer) ;
" Mine is a soul.whose deeper feelings lie
    More deep than words "—(as these exemplify).

43

The Love-Letter.

"I will not say when first your beauty's sun
  Illumed my life,"—(it needs imagination);
"For me to see you and to love were one,"—
  (This will account for some precipitation);
"Let it suffice that worship more devoted
  Ne'er throbbed," *et cætera.* The rest is quoted.

"If Love can look with all-prophetic eye,"—
  (Ah, if he could, how many would be single!),
"If truly spirit unto spirit cry,"—
  (The ears of some most terribly must tingle!)
"Then I have dreamed you will not turn your face."
This next, I think, is more than commonplace.

"Why should we speak, if Love, interpreting,
  Forestall the speech with favour found before?
Why should we plead?—it were an idle thing,
  If Love himself be Love's ambassador!"
Blot, as I live. Shall we erase it? No;—
'T will show we write *currente calamo.*

"My fate,—my fortune, I commit to you,"—
  (In point of fact, the latter 's not extensive);
"Without you I am poor indeed,"—(strike through,
  'T is true but crude—'t would make her apprehen
    sive);

44

" My life is yours—I lay it at your feet,"
  (Having no choice but Hymen or the Fleet).

" Give me the right to stand within the shrine,
    Where never yet my faltering feet intruded ;
  Give me the right to call you wholly mine,"—
    (That is, Consols and Three per Cents included);
" To guard your rest from every care that cankers,—
  To keep your life,"—(and balance at your banker's).

" Compel me not to long for your reply;
    Suspense makes havoc with the mind"—(and
      muscles);
" Winged Hope takes flight,"—(which means that I
      must fly,
    Default of funds, to Paris or to Brussels);
" I cannot wait !　My own, my queen—Priscilla !
  Write by return."　And *now* for a Manilla !

" Miss Blank," at "Blank."　Jemima, let it go ;
    And I, meanwhile, will idle with "Sir Walter ;"
  Stay, let me keep the first rough copy, though—
    'T will serve again.　There 's but the name to alter,
  And Love, — that needs, — must knock at every
      portal,
In formâ pauperis.　We are but mortal !

THE MISOGYNIST.

" Il était un jeune homme d'un bien beau passé."

WHEN first he sought our haunts, he wore
   His locks in Hamlet-style;
His brow with thought was "sicklied o'er,"—
   We rarely saw him smile;
And, e'en when none were looking on,
His air was always woe-begone.

He kept, I think, his bosom bare
   To imitate Jean Paul;
His solitary topics were
   Æsthetics, Fate, and Soul;—
Although at times, but not for long,
He bowed his Intellect to song.

The Misogynist.

He served, he said, a Muse of Tears:
　　I know his verses breathed
A fine funereal air of biers,
　　And objects cypress-wreathed;—
Indeed, his tried acquaintance fled
An ode he named "The Sheeted Dead."

In these light moods, I call to mind,
　　He darkly would allude
To some dread sorrow undefined,—
　　Some passion unsubdued;
Then break into a ghastly laugh,
And talk of Keats his epitaph.

He railed at women's faith as Cant;
　　We thought him grandest when
He named them Siren-shapes that " chant
　　On blanching bones of Men;"—
Alas, not e'en the great go free
From that insidious minstrelsy!

His lot, he oft would gravely urge,
　　Lay on a lone Rock where
Around Time-beaten bases surge
　　The Billows of Despair.
We dreamed it true. We never knew
What gentler ears he told it to.

The Misogynist.

We, bound with him in common care,
  One-minded, celibate,
Resolved to Thought and Diet spare
  Our lives to dedicate;—
We, truly, in no common sense
Deserved his closest confidence!

But soon, and yet, though soon, too late,
  We, sorrowing, sighed to find ·
A gradual softness enervate
  That all superior mind,
Until,—in full assembly met,
He dared to speak of Etiquette.

The verse that we severe had known,
  Assumed a wanton air,—
A fond effeminate monotone
  Of eyebrows, lips, and hair;
Not ἤθος stirred him now or νοῦς,
He read "The Angel in the House!"

Nay worse. He, once sublime to chaff,
  Grew whimsically sore
If we but named a photograph
  We found him simpering o'er;
Or told how in his chambers lurked
A watch-guard intricately worked.

Then worse again.   He tried to dress;
   He trimmed his tragic mane;
Announced at length (to our distress)
   He had not " lived in vain ";—
Thenceforth his one prevailing mood
Became a base beatitude.

And O Jean Paul, and Fate, and Soul!
   We met him last, grown stout,
His throat with wedlock's triple roll,
   " All wool,"—enwound about;
His very hat had changed its brim;—
Our course was clear,—WE BANISHED HIM!

A VIRTUOSO.

Be seated, pray. "A grave appeal"?
   The sufferers by the war, of course;
Ah, what a sight for us who feel,—
   This monstrous *mélodrame* of Force!
We, sir, we connoisseurs, should know,
   On whom its heaviest burden falls;
Collections shattered at a blow,
   Museums turned to hospitals!

"And worse," you say; "the wide distress!"
   Alas, 't is true distress exists,
Though, let me add, our worthy Press
   Have no mean skill as colourists;—
Speaking of colour, next your seat
   There hangs a sketch from Vernet's hand;
Some Moscow fancy, incomplete,
   Yet not indifferently planned;

A Virtuoso.

Note specially the gray old Guard,
    Who tears his tattered coat to wrap
A closer bandage round the scarred
    And frozen comrade in his lap;—
But, as regards the present war,—
    Now don't you think our pride of pence
Goes—may I say it?—somewhat far
    For objects of benevolence?

You hesitate.   For my part, I—
    Though ranking Paris next to Rome,
Æsthetically—still reply
    That "Charity begins at Home."
The words remind me.   Did you catch
    My so-named "Hunt"? The girl 's a gem;
And look how those lean rascals snatch
    The pile of scraps she brings to them!

"But your appeal 's for home,"—you say,—
    For home, and English poor! Indeed!
I thought Philanthropy to-day
    Was blind to mere domestic need—
However sore—Yet though one grants
    That home should have the foremost claims,
At least these Continental wants
    Assume intelligible names;

A Virtuoso.

While here with us—Ah! who could hope
  To verify the varied pleas,
Or from his private means to cope
  With all our shrill necessities!
Impossible!   One might as well
  Attempt comparison of creeds;
Or fill that huge Malayan shell
  With these half-dozen Indian beads.

Moreover, add that every one
  So well exalts his pet distress,
'T is—Give to all, or give to none,
  If you 'd avoid invidiousness.
Your case, I feel, is sad as A.'s,
  The same applies to B.'s and C.'s;
By my selection I should raise
  An alphabet of rivalries;

And life is short,—I see you look
  At yonder dish, a priceless bit;
You 'll find it etched in Jacquemart's book,
  They say that Raphael painted it ;—
And life is short, you understand;
  So, if I only hold you out
An open though an empty hand,
  Why, you 'll forgive me, I 've no doubt.

A Virtuoso.

Nay, do not rise.   You seem amused ;
   One can but be consistent, sir!
'T was on these grounds I just refused
   Some gushing lady-almoner,—
Believe me, on these very grounds.
   Good-bye, then.   Ah, a rarity!
That cost me quite three hundred pounds,—
   That Dürer figure,—"Charity."

LAISSEZ FAIRE.

" Prophete rechts, Prophete links,
   Das Weltkind in der Mitten."
                    —GOETHE'S *Diné zu-Coblenz.*

To left, here 's B., half-Communist,
  Who talks a chastened treason,
And C., a something-else in "ist,"
  Harangues, to right, on Reason.

B., from his "tribune," fulminates
  At Throne and Constitution,
Nay, with the walnuts, advocates
  Reform by revolution;

While C.'s peculiar coterie
  Have now in full rehearsal
Some patent new Philosophy
  To make doubt universal.

Laissez Faire.

And yet—why not ?   If zealots burn,
  Their zeal has not affected
My taste for salmon and Sauterne,
  Or I might have objected :—

Friend B., the argument you choose
  Has been by France refuted ;
And C., *mon cher*, your novel views
  Are just Tom Paine diluted;

There 's but one creed,—that 's *Laissez faire ;*
  Behold its mild apostle !
My dear, declamatory pair,
  Although you shout and jostle,

Not your ephemeral hands, nor mine,
  Time's Gordian knots shall sunder,—
Will. laid three casks of this old wine :
  Who 'll drink the last, I wonder ?

55

TO Q. H. F.

SUGGESTED BY A CHAPTER IN THEODORE MARTIN'S
"HORACE,"

("ANCIENT CLASSICS FOR ENGLISH READERS.")

"HORATIUS FLACCUS, B.C. 8,"
   There 's not a doubt about the date,—
         You 're dead and buried:
   As you observed, the seasons roll;
   And 'cross the Styx full many a soul
         Has Charon ferried,
   Since, mourned of men and Muses nine,
   They laid you on the Esquiline.

   And that was centuries ago!
   You 'd think we 'd learned enough, I know,
         To help refine us,

To Q. H. F.

Since last you trod the Sacred Street,
And tacked from mortal fear to meet
   The bore Crispinus;
Or, by your cold Digentia, set
The web of winter birding-net.

Ours is so far-advanced an age!
Sensation tales, a classic stage,
   Commodious villas!
We boast high art, an Albert Hall,
Australian meats, and men who call
   Their sires gorillas!
We have a thousand things, you see,
Not dreamt in your philosophy.

And yet, how strange! Our "world," to-day,
Tried in the scale, would scarce outweigh
   Your Roman cronies;
Walk in the Park—you 'll seldom fail
To find a Sybaris on the rail
   By Lydia's ponies,
Or hap on Barrus, wigged and stayed,
Ogling some unsuspecting maid.

The great Gargilius, then, behold!
His "long-bow" hunting tales of old
   Are now but duller;

To Q. H. F.

Fair Neobule too!   Is not
One Hebrus here—from Aldershot?
      Aha, you colour!
Be wise.   There old Canidia sits;
No doubt she 's tearing you to bits.

And look, dyspeptic, brave, and kind,
Comes dear Mæcenas, half behind
      Terentia's skirting;
Here 's Pyrrah, "golden-haired" at will;
Prig Damasippus, preaching still;
      Asterie flirting,—
Radiant, of course.   We 'll make her black,—
Ask her when Gyges' ship comes back.

So with the rest.   Who will may trace
Behind the new each elder face
      Defined as clearly;
Science proceeds, and man stands still;
Our "world" to-day 's as good or ill,—
      As cultured (nearly),
As yours was, Horace!   You alone,
Unmatched, unmet, we have not known.

TO "LYDIA LANGUISH."

" Il me faut des émotions."
—BLANCHE AMORY.

You ask me, Lydia, "whether I,
If you refuse my suit, shall die."
   (Now pray don't let this hurt you);
Although the time be out of joint,
I should not think a bodkin's point
   The sole resource of virtue;
Nor shall I, though your mood endure,
Attempt a final Water-cure
   Except against my wishes;
For I respectfully decline
To dignify the Serpentine,
   And make *hors-d'œuvres* for fishes;
But, if you ask me whether I
   Composedly can go,
Without a look, without a sigh,
   Why, then I answer—No.

To "*Lydia Languish.*"

"You are assured," you sadly say
  (If in this most considerate way
    To treat my suit your will is),
That I shall "quickly find as fair
Some new Neæra's tangled hair—
    Some easier Amaryllis."
I cannot promise to be cold
If smiles are kind as yours of old
    On lips of later beauties;
Nor can I hope to quite forget
The homage that is Nature's debt,
    While man has social duties;
But, if you ask shall I prefer
    To you I honour so
A somewhat visionary Her,
    I answer truly—No.

You fear, you frankly add, "to find
In me too late the altered mind
    That altering Time estranges."
To this I make response that we
(As physiologists agree),
    Must have septennial changes;
This is a thing beyond control,
And it were best upon the whole
    To try and find out whether

60

To "Lydia Languish."

We could not, by some means, arrange
This not-to-be-avoided change
  So as to change together:
But, had you asked me to allow
  That you could ever grow
Less amiable than you are now,—
  Emphatically—No.

But—to be serious—if you care
To know how I shall really bear
  This much-discussed rejection,
I answer you. As feeling men
Behave, in best romances, when
  You outrage their affection;—
With that gesticulatory woe,
By which, as melodramas show,
  Despair is indicated;
Enforced by all the liquid grief
Which hugest pocket-handkerchief
  Has ever simulated;
And when, arrived so far, you say
  In tragic accents "Go,"
Then, Lydia, then—I still shall stay,
  And firmly answer No.

A GAGE D'AMOUR.

(HORACE, III, 8.)

" Martiis cælebs quid agam Kalendis,
        ——miraris? "

CHARLES,—for it seems you wish to know,—
You wonder what could scare me so,
And why, in this long-locked bureau,
                With trembling fingers,—
With tragic air, I now replace
This ancient web of yellow lace,
Among whose faded folds the trace
                Of perfume lingers.

Friend of my youth, severe as true,
I guess the train your thoughts pursue;
But this my state is nowise due
                To indigestion;

A Gage d'Amour.

I had forgotten it was there,
A scarf that Some-one used to wear.
Hinc illæ lachrimæ,—so spare
> Your cynic question.

Some-one who is not girlish now,
And wed long since. We meet and bow;
I don't suppose our broken vow
> Affects us keenly;

Yet, trifling though my act appears,
Your Sternes would make it ground for tears;—
One can't disturb the dust of years,
> And smile serenely.

" My golden locks" are gray and chill,
For hers,—let them be sacred still;
But yet, I own, a boyish thrill
> Went dancing through me,

Charles, when I held yon yellow lace;
For, from its dusty hiding-place,
Peeped out an arch, ingenuous face
> That beckoned to me.

We shut our heart up, now-a-days,
Like some old music-box that plays
Unfashionable airs that raise
> Derisive pity;

A Gage d'Amour.

Alas,—a nothing starts the spring;
And lo, the sentimental thing
At once commences quavering
       Its lover's ditty.

Laugh, if you like.   The boy in me,—
The boy that was,—revived to see
The fresh young smile that shone when she,
       Of old, was tender.
Once more we trod the Golden Way,—
That mother you saw yesterday,
And I, whom none can well portray
       As young, or slender.

She twirled the flimsy scarf about
Her pretty head, and stepping out,
Slipped arm in mine, with half a pout
       Of childish pleasure.
Where we were bound no mortal knows,
For then you plunged in Ireland's woes,
And brought me blankly back to prose
       And Gladstone's measure.

Well, well, the wisest bend to Fate.
My brown old books around me wait,
My pipe still holds, unconfiscate,
       Its wonted station.

A Gage d'Amour.

Pass me the wine.   To Those that keep
The bachelor's secluded sleep
Peaceful, inviolate, and deep,
   I pour libation.

CUPID'S ALLEY.

A MORALITY.

O, Love 's but a dance,
*   Where Time plays the fiddle!*
See the couples advance,—
O, Love 's but a dance!
A whisper, a glance,—
*   " Shall we twirl down the middle ? '*
O, Love 's but a dance,
*   Where Time plays the fiddle!*

IT runs (so saith my Chronicler)
    Across a smoky City;—
A Babel filled with buzz and whirr,
    Huge, gloomy, black and gritty;
Dark-louring looks the hill-side near,
    Dark-yawning looks the valley,—
But here 't is always fresh and clear,
    For here—is "Cupid's Alley."

Cupid's Alley.

And, from an Arbour cool and green,
   With aspect down the middle,
An ancient Fiddler, gray and lean,
   Scrapes on an ancient fiddle;
Alert he seems, but aged enow
   To punt the Stygian galley;—
With wisp of forelock on his brow,
   He plays—in "Cupid's Alley."

All day he plays,—a single tune!—
   But, by the oddest chances,
Gavotte, or Brawl, or Rigadoon,
   It suits all kinds of dances;
My Lord may walk a *pas de Cour*
   To Jenny's *pas de Chalet;*—
The folks who ne'er have danced before,
   Can dance—in "Cupid's Alley."

And here, for ages yet untold,
   Long, long before my ditty,
Came high and low, and young and old,
   From out the crowded City;
And still to-day they come, they go,
   And just as fancies tally,
They foot it quick, they foot it slow,
   All day—in "Cupid's Alley."

Cupid's Alley.

Strange dance! 'T is free to Rank and Rags;
    Here no distinction flatters,
Here Riches shakes its money-bags
    And Poverty its tatters;
Church, Army, Navy, Physic, Law;—
    Maid, Mistress, Master, Valet;
Long locks, gray hairs, bald heads, and a',—
    They bob—in "Cupid's Alley."

Strange pairs! To laughing, fresh Fifteen
    Here capers Prudence thrifty;
Here Prodigal leads down the green
    A blushing Maid of fifty;
Some treat it as a serious thing,
    And some but shilly-shally;
And some have danced without the ring
    (Ah me!)—in "Cupid's Alley."

And sometimes one to one will dance,
    And think of one behind her;
And one by one will stand, perchance,
    Yet look all ways to find her;
Some seek a partner with a sigh,
    Some win him with a sally;
And some, they know not how nor why,
    Strange fate!—of "Cupid's Alley."

And some will dance an age or so
    Who came for half a minute;
And some, who like the game, will go
    Before they well begin it;
And some will vow they 're "danced to death,"
    Who (somehow) always rally;
Strange cures are wrought (mine author saith),
    Strange cures!—in "Cupid's Alley."

It may be one will dance to-day,
    And dance no more to-morrow;
It may be one will steal away
    And nurse a life-long sorrow;
What then?   The rest advance, evade,
    Unite, dispart, and dally,
Re-set, coquet, and gallopade,
    Not less—in "Cupid's Alley."

For till that City's wheel-work vast
    And shuddering beams shall crumble;—
And till that Fiddler lean at last
    From off his seat shall tumble;—
Till then (the Civic records say),
    This quaint, fantastic *ballet*
Of Go and Stay, of Yea and Nay,
    Must last—in "Cupid's Alley."

THE IDYLL OF THE CARP.

(The Scene is in a garden,—where you please,
   So that it lie in France, and have withal
Its gray-stoned pond beneath the arching trees,
   And Triton huge, with moss for coronal.
A PRINCESS,—feeding Fish. To her DENISE.)

THE PRINCESS.

These, DENISE, are my Suitors!

DENISE.

               Where?

THE PRINCESS.

             These fish.
I feed them daily here at morn and night
With crumbs of favour,—scraps of graciousness,
Not meant, indeed, to mean the thing they wish,
But serving just to edge an appetite.
        (Throwing bread.)
Make haste, *Messieurs!* Make haste, then! Hurry.
   See,—

See how they swim!   Would you not say, confess,
Some crowd of Courtiers in the audience hall,
When the King comes?

DENISE.
You 're jesting!

THE PRINCESS.
Not at all.

Watch but the great one yonder!   There 's the
 Duke;—
Those gill-marks mean his Order of St. Luke;
Those old skin-stains his boasted quarterings.
Look what a swirl and roll of tide he brings;
Have you not marked him thus, with crest in air,
Breathing disdain, descend the palace-stair?
You surely have, DENISE.

DENISE.
I think I have.

But there 's another, older and more grave,—
The one that wears the round patch on the throat
And swims with such slow fins.   Is he of note?

THE PRINCESS.
Why that 's my good *chambellan*—with his seal.
A kind old man!—he carves me orange-peel

The Idyll of the Carp.

In quaint devices at refection-hours,
Equips my sweet-pouch, brings me morning flowers
Or chirrups madrigals with old, sweet words,
Such as men loved when people wooed like birds
And spoke the true note first.   No suitor he,
Yet loves me too,—though in a graybeard's key.

DENISE.

Look, Madam, look!—a fish without a stain!
O speckless, fleckless fish!   Who is it pray,
That bears him so discreetly?

THE PRINCESS.
FONTENAY.

You know him not?   My prince of shining locks!
My pearl!—my Phœnix!—my pomander-box!
He loves not Me, alas!   The man 's too vain!
He loves his doublet better than my suit,—
His graces than my favours.   Still his sash
Sits not amiss, and he can touch the lute
Not wholly out of tune—

DENISE.
                    Ai! what a splash!
Who is it comes with such a sudden dash
Plump i' the midst, and leaps the others clear?

The Idyll of the Carp.

THE PRINCESS.

Ho! for a trumpet! Let the bells be rung!
Baron of *Sans-terre*, Lord of *Prés-en-Cieux*,
Vidame of *Vol-au-Vent*—"*et aultres lieux!*"
Bah! How I hate his Gasconading tongue!
Why, that 's my bragging, Bravo-Musketeer—
My carpet cut-throat, valiant by a scar
Got in a brawl that stands for Spanish war :—
His very life 's a splash!

DENISE.
    I 'd rather wear
E'en such a patched and melancholy air,
As his,—that motley one,—who keeps the wall,
And hugs his own lean thoughts for carnival.

THE PRINCESS,

My frankest wooer! Thus *his* love he tells
To mournful moving of his cap and bells.
He loves me (so he saith) as Slaves the Free,—
As Cowards War,—as young Maids Constancy.
Item, he loves me as the Hawk the Dove;
He loves me as the Inquisition Thought;—

DENISE.
"He loves?—he loves?" Why all this loving 's
  naught!

The Idyll of the Carp.

THE PRINCESS.

And " Naught (quoth JACQUOT) makes the sum of
    Love !"

DENISE.

The cynic knave !   How call you this one here ?—
This small shy-looking fish, that hovers near,
And circles, like a cat around a cage,
To snatch the surplus.

THE PRINCESS.

               CHÉRUBIN, the page.
'T is but a child, yet with that roguish smile,
And those sly looks, the child will make hearts ache
Not five years hence, I prophesy.   Meanwhile
He lives to plague the swans upon the lake,
To steal my comfits, and the monkey's cake.

DENISE.

And these—that swim aside—who may these be ?

THE PRINCESS.

Those—are two gentlemen of Picardy,
Equal in blood,—of equal bravery :—
D'AURELLES and MAUFRIGNAC.   They hunt in pairs;
I mete them morsels with an equal care,
Lest they should eat each other,—or eat Me.

The Idyll of the Carp.

DENISE.

And that—and that—and that?

THE PRINCESS.

I name them not.
Those are the crowd who merely think their lot
The lighter by my land.

DENISE.

And is there none
More prized than most? There surely must be one,--
A Carp of carps!

THE PRINCESS.

Ah me!—he will not come!
He swims at large,—looks shyly on,—is dumb.
Sometimes, indeed, I think he fain would nibble,
But while he stays with doubts and fears to quibble,
Some gilded fop, or mincing courtier-fribble,
Slips smartly in,—and gets the proffered crumb.
He should have all my crumbs—if he 'd but ask;
Nay, an he would, it were no hopeless task
To gain a something more. But though he 's brave,
He 's far too proud to be a dangling slave;
And then—he 's modest! So . . . he will not come!

75

THE SUNDIAL.

'T is an old dial, dark with many a stain;
  In summer crowned with drifting orchard bloom,
Tricked in the autumn with the yellow rain,
  And white in winter like a marble tomb;

And round about its gray, time-eaten brow
  Lean letters speak—a worn and shattered row:
𝕴 am a 𝕾𝖍𝖆𝖉𝖊: a 𝕾𝖍𝖆𝖉𝖔𝖜𝖊 too arte thou:
  𝕴 marke the 𝕿ime: saye, 𝕲ossip, dost thou
    soe?

Here would the ringdoves linger, head to head;
  And here the snail a silver course would run,
Beating old Time; and here the peacock spread
  His gold-green glory, shutting out the sun.

The Sundial.

The tardy shade moved forward to the noon;
   Betwixt the paths a dainty Beauty stept,
That swung a flower, and, smiling, hummed a tune,—
   Before whose feet a barking spaniel leapt.

O'er her blue dress an endless blossom strayed;
   About her tendril-curls the sunlight shone;
And round her train the tiger-lilies swayed,
   Like courtiers bowing till the queen be gone.

She leaned upon the slab a little while,
   Then drew a jewelled pencil from her zone,
Scribbled a something with a frolic smile,
   Folded, inscribed, and niched it in the stone.

The shade slipped on, no swifter than the snail;
   There came a second lady to the place,
Dove-eyed, dove-robed, and something wan and pale—
   An inner beauty shining from her face.

She, as if listless with a lonely love,
   Straying among the alleys with a book,—
Herrick or Herbert,—watched the circling dove,
   And spied the tiny letter in the nook.

The Sundial.

Then, like to one who confirmation found
    Of some dread secret half-accounted true,—
Who knew what hands and hearts the letter bound,
    And argued loving commerce 'twixt the two,

She bent her fair young forehead on the stone;
    The dark shade gloomed an instant on her head;
And 'twixt her taper-fingers pearled and shone
    The single tear that tear-worn eyes will shed.

The shade slipped onward to the falling gloom;
    There came a soldier gallant in her stead,
Swinging a beaver with a swaling plume,
    A ribboned love-lock rippling from his head;

Blue-eyed, frank-faced, with clear and open brow,
    Scar-seamed a little, as the women love;
So kindly fronted that you marvelled how
    The frequent sword-hilt had so frayed his glove;

Who switched at Psyche plunging in the sun;
    Uncrowned three lilies with a backward swinge;
And standing somewhat widely, like to one
    More used to "Boot and Saddle" than to cringe

As courtiers do, but gentleman withal,
  Took out the note;—held it as one who feared
The fragile thing he held would slip and fall;
  Read and re-read, pulling his tawny beard;

Kissed it, I think, and hid it in his breast;
  Laughed softly in a flattered happy way,
Arranged the broidered baldrick on his chest,
  And sauntered past, singing a roundelay.

    .   .   .   .   .   .

The shade crept forward through the dying glow;
  There came no more nor dame nor cavalier;
But for a little time the brass will show
  A small gray spot—the record of a tear.

79

AN UNFINISHED SONG.

" Cantat Deo qui vivit Deo."

YES, he was well-nigh gone and near his rest,
  The year could not renew him; nor the cry
Of building nightingales about the nest;
  Nor that soft freshness of the May-wind's sigh,

That fell before the garden scents, and died
  Between the ampler leafage of the trees :
All these he knew not, lying open-eyed,
  Deep in a dream that was not pain nor ease,

But death not yet.   Outside a woman talked—
  His wife she was—whose clicking needles sped
To faded phrases of complaint that balked
  My rising words of comfort.   Overhead,

An Unfinished Song.

A cage that hung amid the jasmine stars
   Trembled a little, and a blossom dropped.
Then notes came pouring through the wicker bars,
   Climbed half a rapid arc of song, and stopped.

"Is it a thrush?" I asked. "A thrush," she said.
   "That was Will's tune. Will taught him that before
He left the doorway settle for his bed,
   Sick as you see, and could n't teach him more.

"He 'd bring his Bible here o' nights, would Will,
   Following the light, and whiles when it was dark
And days were warm, he 'd sit there whistling still,
   Teaching the bird. He whistled like a lark."

"Jack! Jack!" A joyous flutter stirred the cage,
   Shaking the blossoms down. The bird began;
The woman turned again to want and wage,
   And in the inner chamber sighed the man.

How clear the song was! Musing as I heard,
   My fancies wandered from the droning wife
To sad comparison of man and bird,—
   The broken song, the uncompleted life,

An Unfinished Song.

That seemed a broken song; and of the two,
　　My thought a moment deemed the bird more
　　　　blest,
That, when the sun shone, sang the notes it knew,
　　Without desire or knowledge of the rest.

Nay, happier man.　For him futurity
　　Still hides a hope that this his earthly praise
Finds heavenly end, for surely will not He,
　　Solver of all, above his Flower of Days,

Teach him the song that no one living knows?
　　Let the man die, with that half-chant of his,—
What Now discovers not Hereafter shows,
　　And God will surely teach him more than this.

Again the Bird.　I turned, and passed along;
　　But Time and Death, Eternity and Change,
Talked with me ever, and the climbing song
　　Rose in my hearing, beautiful and strange.

82

THE CHILD-MUSICIAN.

He had played for his lordship's levee,
  He had played for her ladyship's whim,
Till the poor little head was heavy,
  And the poor little brain would swim.

And the face grew peaked and eerie,
  And the large eyes strange and bright,
And they said—too late—"He is weary!
  He shall rest for, at least, To-night!"

But at dawn, when the birds were waking,
  As they watched in the silent room,
With the sound of a strained cord breaking,
  A something snapped in the gloom.

'T was a string of his violoncello,
  And they heard him stir in his bed:—
"Make room for a tired little fellow,
  Kind God!—" was the last that he said.

THE CRADLE.

How steadfastly she 'd worked at it!
  How lovingly had drest
With all her would-be-mother's wit
  That little rosy nest!

How longingly she 'd hung on it!—
  It sometimes seemed, she said,
There lay beneath its coverlet
  A little sleeping head.

He came at last, the tiny guest,
  Ere bleak December fled;
That rosy nest he never prest . . . .
  Her coffin was his bed.

BEFORE SEDAN.

" The dead hand clasped a letter."
　　　　　—Special Correspondence.

Here, in this leafy place,
　　Quiet he lies,
Cold, with his sightless face
　　Turned to the skies;
'T is but another dead;
All you can say is said.

Carry his body hence,—
　　Kings must have slaves;
Kings climb to eminence
　　Over men's graves:
So this man's eye is dim;—
Throw the earth over him.

What was the white you touched,
　　There, at his side?

Before Sedan.

Paper his hand had clutched
    Tight ere he died;—
Message or wish, may be;—
Smooth the folds out and see.

Hardly the worst of us
    Here could have smiled!—
Only the tremulous
    Words of a child;—
Prattle, that has for stops
Just a few ruddy drops.

Look.   She is sad to miss,
    Morning and night,
His—her dead father's—kiss;
    Tries to be bright,
Good to mamma, and sweet.
That is all. "Marguerite."

Ah, if beside the dead
    Slumbered the pain!
Ah, if the hearts that bled
    Slept with the slain!
If the grief died;—But no;—
Death will not have it so.

THE FORGOTTEN GRAVE.

A SKETCH IN A CEMETERY.

OUT from the City's dust and roar,
You wandered through the open door;
Paused at a plaything pail and spade
Across a tiny hillock laid;
Then noted on your dexter side
Some moneyed mourner's "love or pride";
And so,—beyond a hawthorn-tree,
Showering its rain of rosy bloom
Alike on low and lofty tomb,—
You came upon it—suddenly.

How strange!   The very grasses' growth
Around it seemed forlorn and loath;
The very ivy seemed to turn
Askance that wreathed the neighbour urn.

The Forgotten Grave.

The slab had sunk; the head declined,
And left the rails a wreck behind.
No name; you traced a " 6,"—a " 7,"—
Part of "affliction" and of " Heaven";
And then, in letters sharp and clear,
You read—O Irony austere !—
" *Tho' lost to Sight, to Memory dear.*"

MY LANDLADY.

A SMALL brisk woman, capped with many a bow;
  "Yes," so she says, "and younger, too, than some,"
Who bids me, bustling, "God speed," when I go,
    And gives me, rustling, "Welcome" when I come.

" Ay, sir, 't is cold,—and freezing hard,—they say;
    I 'd like to give that hulking brute a hit—
Beating his horse in such a shameful way!—
    Step here, sir, till your fire 's blazed up a bit."

A musky haunt of lavender and shells,
    Quaint-figured Chinese monsters, toys, and trays—
A life's collection—where each object tells
    Of fashions gone and half-forgotten ways:—

A glossy screen, where wide-mouth dragons ramp;
    A vexed inscription in a sampler-frame;
A shade of beads upon a red-capped lamp;
    A child's mug graven with a golden name;

89

My Landlady.

A pictured ship, with full-blown canvas set;
  A cord, with sea-weed twisted to a wreath,
Circling a silky curl as black as jet,
  With yellow writing faded underneath.

Looking, I sink within the shrouded chair,
  And note the objects slowly, one by one,
And light at last upon a portrait there,—
  Wide-collared, raven-haired. "Yes, 't is my son!"

"Where is he?" "Ah, sir, he is dead—my boy!
  Nigh ten long years ago—in 'sixty-three;
He 's always living in my head—my boy!
  He was left drowning in the Southern Sea.

"There were two souls washed overboard, they said,
  And one the waves brought back; but he was left.
They saw him place the life-buoy o'er his head;
  The sea was running wildly;—he was left.

"He was a strong, strong swimmer. Do you know,
  When the wind whistled yesternight, I cried,
And prayed to God . . . though 't was so long ago,
  He did not struggle much before he died.

" 'T was his third voyage. That 's the box he
    brought,—
Or would have brought—my poor deserted boy !
And these the words the agents sent—they thought
    That money, perhaps, could make my loss a joy.

" Look, sir, I 've something here that I prize more :
    This is a fragment of the poor lad's coat,—
That other clutched him as the wave went o'er,
    And this stayed in his hand. That 's what they
    wrote.

" Well, well, 't is done. My story 's shocking you ;—
    Grief is for them that have both time and wealth :
We can't mourn much, who have much work to do ;
    Your fire is bright. Thank God, I have my
    health !"

91

AT THE CONVENT GATE.

WISTARIA blossoms trail and fall
Above the length of barrier wall;
    And softly, now and then,
The shy, staid-breasted doves will flit
From roof to gateway-top, and sit
    And watch the ways of men.

The gate 's ajar.   If one might peep!
Ah, what a haunt of rest and sleep
    The shadowy garden seems!
And note how dimly to and fro
The grave, gray-hooded Sisters go,
    Like figures seen in dreams.

Look, there is one that tells her beads;
And yonder one apart that reads
    A tiny missal's page;

At the Convent Gate.

And see, beside the well, the two
That, kneeling, strive to lure anew
 The magpie to its cage!

Not beautiful—not all! But each
With that mild grace, outlying speech,
 Which comes of even mood;—
The Veil unseen that women wear
With heart-whole thought, and quiet care,
 And hope of higher good.

"A placid life—a peaceful life!
What need to these the name of Wife?
 What gentler task (I said)—
What worthier—e'en your arts among—
Than tend the sick, and teach the young,
 And give the hungry bread?"

"No worthier task!" re-echoes She,
Who (closelier clinging) turns with me
 To face the road again:
—And yet, in that warm heart of hers,
She means the doves', for she prefers
 To "watch the ways of men."

THE CURÉ'S PROGRESS.

MONSIEUR the Curé down the street
    Comes with his kind old face,—
With his coat worn bare, and his straggling hair,
    And his green umbrella-case.

You may see him pass by the little "*Grande Place,*"
    And the tiny "*Hôtel-de-Ville*";
He smiles as he goes, to the *fleuriste* Rose,
    And the *pompier* Théophile.

He turns, as a rule, through the "*Marché*" cool,
    Where the noisy fish-wives call;
And his compliments pays to the "*belle Thérèse,*"
    As she knits in her dusky stall.

There 's a letter to drop at the locksmith's shop,
    And Toto, the locksmith's niece,
Has jubilant hopes, for the Curé gropes
    In his tails for a *pain d'épice.*

The Curé's Progress.

There 's a little dispute with a merchant of fruit,
    Who is said to be heterodox,
That will ended be with a "*Ma foi, oui!*"
    And a pinch from the Curé's box.

There is also a word that no one heard
    To the furrier's daughter Lou.;
And a pale cheek fed with a flickering red,
    And a "*Bon Dieu garde M'sieu!*"

But a grander way for the *Sous-Préfet*,
    And a bow for Ma'am'selle Anne;
And a mock "off-hat" to the Notary's cat,
    And a nod to the Sacristan :—

For ever through life the Curé goes
    With a smile on his kind old face—
With his coat worn bare, and his straggling hair,
    And his green umbrella-case.

95

AN OLD FISH-POND.

GREEN growths of mosses drop and bead
   Around the granite brink;
And 'twixt the isles of water-weed
   The wood-birds dip and drink.

Slow efts about the edges sleep;
   Swift-darting water-flies
Shoot on the surface; down the deep
   Fast-following bubbles rise.

Look down.   What groves that scarcely sway!
   What "wood obscure," profound!
What jungle!—where some beast of prey
   Might choose a vantage-ground!

.   .   .   .   .   .

Who knows what lurks beneath the tide?—
   Who knows what tale?   Belike,
Those "antres vast" and shadows hide
   Some patriarchal Pike;—

An Old Fish-Pond.

Some tough old tyrant, wrinkle-jawed,
    To whom the sky, the earth,
Have but for aim to look on awed
    And see him wax in girth;—

Hard ruler there by right of might;
    An ageless Autocrat,
Whose "good old rule" is "Appetite,
    And subjects fresh and fat;"—

While they—poor souls!—in wan despair
    Still watch for signs in him;
And dying, hand from heir to heir
    The day undawned and dim,

When the pond's terror too must go;
    Or creeping in by stealth,
Some bolder brood, with common blow,
    Shall found a Commonwealth.

   .   .   .   .   .   .

Or say,—perchance the liker this!—
    That these themselves are gone;—
That Amurath *in minimis*,—
    Still hungry,—lingers on,

An Old Fish-Pond.

With dwindling trunk and wolfish jaw
   Revolving sullen things,
But most the blind unequal law
   That rules the food of Kings;—

The blot that makes the cosmic All
   A mere time-honored cheat;—
That bids the Great to eat the Small,
   Yet lack the Small to eat!

  .   .   .   .   .   .

Who knows!   Meanwhile the mosses bead
   Around the granite brink;
And 'twixt the isles of water-weed
   The wood-birds dip and drink.

BEFORE THE CURTAIN.

"MISS PEACOCK 's called."   And who demurs ?
   Not I who write, for certain;
If praise be due, one sure prefers
That some such face as fresh as hers
   Should come before the curtain.

And yet, most strange to say, I find
   (E'en bards are sometimes prosy)
Her presence here but brings to mind
That undistinguished crowd behind
   For whom life 's not so rosy.

The pleased young *premier* led her on,
   But where are all the others ?
Where is that nimble servant John ?
And where 's the comic Uncle gone ?
   And where that best of Mothers ?

Where is "Sir Lumley Leycester, Bart." ?
   And where the crafty Cousin ?—

Before the Curtain.

That man may have a kindly heart,
And yet each night ('t is in the part)
  Must poison half-a-dozen!

Where is the cool Detective,—he
  Should surely be applauded?
The Lawyer, who refused the fee?
The Wedding Guests (in number three)?—
  Why are they all defrauded?

The men who worked the cataract?
  The plush-clad carpet lifters?—
Where is the countless host, in fact,
Whose cue is not to speak, but act,—
  The "supers" and the shifters?

Think what a crowd whom none recall,
  Unsung,—unpraised,—unpitied;—
Women for whom no bouquets fall,
And men whose names no galleries bawl,—
  The Great un-Benefit-ed!

Ah, Reader, ere you turn the page,
  I leave you this for Moral:—
Remember those who tread Life's stage
With weary feet and scantest wage,
  And ne'er a leaf for laurel!

A NIGHTINGALE IN KENSINGTON GARDENS.

THEY paused,—the cripple in the chair,
　　More bent with pain than age;
The mother with her lines of care;
　　The many-buttoned page;

The noisy, red-cheeked nursery-maid,
　　With straggling train of three;
The Frenchman with his frogs and braid;—
　　All, curious, paused to see,

If possible, the small, dusk bird
　　That from the almond bough,
Had poured the joyous chant they heard,
　　So suddenly, but now.

A Nightingale in Kensington Garden.

And one poor POET stopped and thought—
    How many a lonely lay
That bird had sung ere fortune brought
    It near the common way,

Where the crowd hears the note.   And then,—
    What birds must sing the song,
To whom that hour of listening men
    Could ne'er in life belong!

But "Art for Art!" the Poet said,
  "'T is still the Nightingale,
That sings where no men's feet will tread,
    And praise and audience fail."

POEMS OF THE EIGHTEENTH CENTURY

(ENGLISH)

A DEAD LETTER.

" A cœur blessé—l'ombre et le silence."
—H. DE BALZAC.

I.

I DREW it from its china tomb;—
    It came out feebly scented
With some thin ghost of past perfume
    That time and years had lent it.

An old, old letter,—folded still!
    To read with due composure
I sought the sun-lit window-sill
    Above the gray enclosure,

That, glimmering in the sultry haze,
    Faint-flowered, dimly shaded,
Slumbered, like Goldsmith's Madam Blaize,
    Bedizened and brocaded.

A Dead Letter.

A queer old place! You 'd surely say
  Some tea-board garden-maker
Had planned it in Dutch William's day
  To please some florist Quaker,

So trim it was. The yew-trees still,
  With pious care perverted,
Grew in the same grim shapes; and still
  The lipless dolphin spurted;

Still in his wonted state abode
  The broken-nosed Apollo;
And still the cypress-arbour showed
  The same umbrageous hollow.

Only,—as fresh young Beauty gleams
  From coffee-coloured laces,—
So peeped from its old-fashioned dreams
  The fresher modern traces;

For idle mallet, hoop, and ball
  Upon the lawn were lying;
A magazine, a tumbled shawl,
  Round which the swifts were flying;

And, tossed beside the Guelder rose,
   A heap of rainbow knitting,
Where, blinking in her pleased repose,
   A Persian cat was sitting.

"A place to love in,—live,—for aye,
   If we too, like Tithonus,
Could find some God to stretch the gray,
   Scant life the Fates have thrown us;

"But now by steam we run our race
   With buttoned heart and pocket;
Our Love 's a gilded, surplus grace,—
   Just like an empty locket.

"'The time is out of joint.' Who will,
   May strive to make it better;
For me, this warm old window-sill,
   And this old dusty letter."

II.

"Dear *John* (the letter ran), it can't, can't be,
   For Father 's gone to *Chorley Fair* with *Sam,*
And Mother 's storing Apples,—*Prue* and Me
   Up to our Elbows making Damson Jam:

But we shall meet before a Week is gone,—
'"T is a long Lane that has no Turning,' *John!*

" Only till Sunday next, and then you 'll wait
  Behind the White-Thorn, by the broken Stile—
We can go round and catch them at the Gate,
  All to ourselves, for nearly one long Mile;
Dear *Prue* won't look, and Father he 'll go on,
And *Sam's* two Eyes are all for *Cissy*, *John!*

" *John*, she 's so smart,—with every Ribbon new,
  Flame-coloured Sack, and Crimson Padesoy;
As proud as proud; and has the Vapours too,
  Just like My Lady;—calls poor *Sam* a boy,
And vows no Sweet-Heart 's worth the Thinking-on
Till he 's past Thirty . . . I know better, *John!*

" My Dear, I don't think that I thought of much
  Before we knew each other, I and you;
And now, why, *John*, your least, least Finger-touch,
  Gives me enough to think a Summer through.
See, for I send you Something! There, 't is gone!
Look in this corner,—mind you find it, *John!*"

III.

This was the matter of the note,—
 A long-forgot deposit,

A Dead Letter.

Dropped in an Indian dragon's throat,
    Deep in a fragrant closet,

Piled with a dapper Dresden world,—
    Beaux, beauties, prayers, and poses,—
Bronzes with squat legs undercurled,
    And great jars filled with roses.

Ah, heart that wrote!   Ah, lips that kissed!
    You had no thought or presage
Into what keeping you dismissed
    Your simple old-world message!

A reverent one.   Though we to-day
    Distrust beliefs and powers,
The artless, ageless things you say
    Are fresh as May's own flowers,

Starring some pure primeval spring,
    Ere Gold had grown despotic,—
Ere Life was yet a selfish thing,
    Or Love a mere exotic.

I need not search too much to find
    Whose lot it was to send it,

A Dead Letter.

That feel upon me yet the kind,
   Soft hand of her who penned it;

And see, through two score years of smoke,
   In by-gone, quaint apparel,
Shine from yon time-black Norway oak
   The face of Patience Caryl,—

The pale, smooth forehead, silver-tressed;
   The gray gown, primly flowered;
The spotless, stately coif whose crest
   Like Hector's horse-plume towered;

And still the sweet half-solemn look
   Where some past thought was clinging,
As when one shuts a serious book
   To hear the thrushes singing.

I kneel to you! Of those you were,
   Whose kind old hearts grow mellow,—
Whose fair old faces grow more fair
   As Point and Flanders yellow;

Whom some old store of garnered grief,
   Their placid temples shading,

A Dead Letter.

Crowns like a wreath of autumn leaf
  With tender tints of fading.

Peace to your soul!   You died unwed—
  Despite this loving letter.
And what of John ?   The less that 's said
  Of John, I think, the better.

A GENTLEMAN OF THE OLD SCHOOL.

HE lived in that past Georgian day,
When men were less inclined to say
That "Time is Gold," and overlay
    With toil their pleasure;
He held some land, and dwelt thereon,—
Where, I forget,—the house is gone;
His Christian name, I think, was John,—
    His surname, Leisure.

Reynolds has painted him,—a face
Filled with a fine, old-fashioned grace,
Fresh-coloured, frank, with ne'er a trace
    Of trouble shaded;
The eyes are blue, the hair is drest
In plainest way,—one hand is prest
Deep in a flapped canary vest,
    With buds brocaded.

A Gentleman of the Old School.

He wears a brown old Brunswick coat,
With silver buttons,—round his throat,
A soft cravat;—in all you note
      An elder fashion,—
A strangeness, which, to us who shine
In shapely hats,—whose coats combine
All harmonies of hue and line,
      Inspires compassion.

He lived so long ago, you see;
Men were untravelled then, but we,
Like Ariel, post o'er land and sea
      With careless parting;
He found it quite enough for him
To smoke his pipe in "garden trim,"
And watch, about the fish tank's brim,
      The swallows darting.

He liked the well-wheel's creaking tongue,—
He liked the thrush that stopped and sung,—
He liked the drone of flies among
      His netted peaches;
He liked to watch the sunlight fall
Athwart his ivied orchard wall;
Or pause to catch the cuckoo's call
      Beyond the beeches.

A Gentleman of the Old School.

His were the times of Paint and Patch,
Aud yet no Ranelagh could match
The sober doves that round his thatch
      Spread tails and sidled;
He liked their ruffling, puffed content,—
For him their drowsy wheelings meant
More than a Mall of Beaux that bent,
      Or Belles that bridled.

Not that, in truth, when life began
He shunned the flutter of the fan;
He too had may be "pinked his man"
      In Beauty's quarrel;
But now his "fervent youth" had flown
Where lost things go; and he was grown
As staid and slow-paced as his own
      Old hunter, Sorrel.

Yet still he loved the chase, and held
That no composer's score excelled
The merry horn, when Sweetlip swelled
      Its jovial riot;
But most his measured words of praise
Caressed the angler's easy ways,—
His idly meditative days,—
      His rustic diet.

Not that his "meditating" rose
Beyond a sunny summer doze;
He never troubled his repose
      With fruitless prying;
But held, as law for high and low,
What God conceals no man can know,
And smiled away inquiry so,
      Without replying.

We read—alas, how much we read!—
The jumbled strifes of creed and creed
With endless controversies feed
      Our groaning tables;
His books—and they sufficed him—were
Cotton's "Montaigne," "The Grave" of Blair,
A "Walton"—much the worse for wear,
      And "Æsop's Fables."

One more,—"The Bible." Not that he
Had searched its page as deep as we;
No sophistries could make him see
      Its slender credit;
It may be that he could not count
The sires and sons to Jesse's fount,—
He liked the "Sermon on the Mount,"—
      And more, he read it.

A Gentleman of the Old School.

Once he had loved, but failed to wed,
A red-cheeked lass who long was dead;
His ways were far too slow, he said,
　　　To quite forget her;
And still when time had turned him gray,
The earliest hawthorn buds in May
Would find his lingering feet astray,
　　　Where first he met her.

" *In Cœlo Quies*" heads the stone
On Leisure's grave,—now little known,
A tangle of wild-rose has grown
　　　So thick across it;
The " Benefactions" still declare
He left the clerk an elbow-chair,
And " 12 Pence Yearly to Prepare
　　　A Christmas Posset."

Lie softly, Leisure!　Doubtless you,
With too serene a conscience drew
Your easy breath, and slumbered through
　　　The gravest issue;
But we, to whom our age allows
Scarce space to wipe our weary brows,
Look down upon your narrow house,
　　　Old friend, and miss you!

A GENTLEWOMAN OF THE OLD SCHOOL.

SHE lived in Georgian era too.
Most women then, if bards be true,
Succumbed to Routs and Cards, or grew
      Devout or acid.
But hers was neither fate.   She came
Of good west-country folk, whose fame
Has faded now.   For us her name
      Is "Madam Placid."

Patience or Prudence,—what you will,
Some prefix faintly fragrant still
As those old musky scents that fill
      Our grandams' pillows;
And for her youthful portrait take
Some long-waist child of Hudson's make,
Stiffly at ease beside a lake
      With swans and willows.

A Gentlewoman of the Old School.

I keep her later semblance placed
Beside my desk,—'t is lawned and laced,
In shadowy sanguine stipple traced
    By Bartolozzi;
A placid face, in which surprise
Is seldom seen, but yet there lies
Some vestige of the laughing eyes
    Of arch Piozzi.

For her e'en Time grew debonair.
He, finding cheeks unclaimed of care,
With late-delayed faint roses there,
    And lingering dimples,
Had spared to touch the fair old face,
And only kissed with Vauxhall grace
The soft white hand that stroked her lace,
    Or smoothed her wimples.

So left her beautiful.   Her age
Was comely as her youth was sage,
And yet she once had been the rage;—
    It hath been hinted,
Indeed, affirmed by one or two,
Some spark at Bath (as sparks will do)
Inscribed a song to "Lovely Prue,"
    Which Urban printed.

A Gentlewoman of the Old School.

I know she thought; I know she felt;
Perchance could sum, I doubt she spelt,
She knew as little of the Celt
      As of the Saxon;
I know she played and sang, for yet
We keep the tumble-down spinet
To which she quavered ballads set
      By Arne or Jackson.

Her tastes were not refined as ours,
She liked plain food and homely flowers,
Refused to paint, kept early hours,
      Went clad demurely;
Her art was sampler-work design,
Fireworks for her were "vastly fine,"
Her luxury was elder-wine,—
      She loved that "purely."

She was renowned, traditions say,
For June conserves, for curds and whey,
For finest tea (she called it "tay"),
      And ratafia;
She knew, for sprains, what bands to choose,
Could tell the sovereign wash to use
For freckles, and was learned in brews
      As erst Medea.

Yet studied little.   She would read,
On Sundays, "Pearson on the Creed,"
Though, as I think, she could not heed
      His text profoundly;
Seeing she chose for her retreat
The warm west-looking window-seat,
Where, if you chanced to raise your feet,
      You slumbered soundly.

This, 'twixt ourselves.   The dear old dame,
In truth, was not so much to blame;
The excellent divine I name
      Is scarcely stirring;
Her plain-song piety preferred
Pure life to precept.   If she erred,
She knew her faults.   Her softest word
      Was for the erring.

If she had loved, or if she kept
Some ancient memory green, or wept
Over the shoulder-knot that slept
      Within her cuff-box,
I know not.   Only this I know,
At sixty-five she 'd still her beau,
A lean French exile, lame and slow,
      With monstrous snuff-box.

A Gentlewoman of the Old School.

Younger than she, well-born and bred.
She 'd found him in St. Giles', half dead
Of teaching French for nightly bed
       And daily dinners;
Starving, in fact, 'twixt want and pride;
And so, henceforth, you always spied
His rusty "pigeon-wings" beside
       Her Mechlin pinners.

He worshipped her, you may suppose.
She gained him pupils, gave him clothes,
Delighted in his dry bon-mots
       And cackling laughter;
And when, at last, the long duet
Of conversation and picquet
Ceased with her death, of sheer regret
       He died soon after.

Dear Madam Placid! Others knew
Your worth as well as he, and threw
Their flowers upon your coffin too,
       I take for granted.
Their loves are lost; but still we see
Your kind and gracious memory
Bloom yearly with the almond tree
       The Frenchman planted.

A CHAPTER OF FROISSART.

You don't know Froissart now, young folks.
  This age, I think, prefers recitals
Of high-spiced crime, with "slang" for jokes,
          And startling titles;

But, in my time, when still some few
  Loved "old Montaigne," and praised Pope's *Homer*
(Nay, thought to style him "poet" too,
          Were scarce misnomer),

Sir John was less ignored.   Indeed,
  I can re-call how Some-one present
(Who spoils her grandson, Frank!) would read,
          And find him pleasant;

122

A Chapter of Froissart.

For,—by this copy,—hangs a Tale.
  Long since, in an old house in Surrey,
Where men knew more of "morning ale"
        Than "Lindley Murray,"

In a dim-lighted, whip-hung hall,
  'Neath Hogarth's "Midnight Conversation"
It stood; and oft 'twixt spring and fall,
        With fond elation,

I turned the brown old leaves. For there
  All through one hopeful happy summer,
At such a page (I well knew where),
        Some secret comer,

Whom I can picture, 'Trix, like you
  (Though scarcely such a colt unbroken),
Would sometimes place for private view
        A certain token ;—

A rose-leaf meaning "Garden Wall,"
  An ivy-leaf for "Orchard corner,"
A thorn to say " Don't come at all,"—
        Unwelcome warner!—

123

A Chapter of Froissart.

Not that, in truth, our friends gainsaid;
  But then Romance required dissembling,
(Ann Radcliffe taught us that!) which bred
          Some genuine trembling;—

Though, as a rule, all used to end
  In such kind confidential parley
As may to you kind Fortune send,
          You long-legged Charlie,

When your time comes.   How years slip on!
  We had our crosses like our betters;
Fate sometimes looked askance upon
          Those floral letters;

And once, for three long days disdained,
  The dust upon the folio settled;
For some-one, in the right, was pained,
          And some-one nettled,

That sure was in the wrong, but spake
  Of fixed intent and purpose stony
To serve King George, enlist and make
          Minced-meat of "Boney,"

A Chapter of Froissart.

Who yet survived—ten years at least.
 And so, when she I mean came hither,
One day that need for letters ceased,
    She brought this with her!

Here is the leaf-stained Chapter:—*How*
 The English King laid Siege to Calais;
I think Gran. knows it even now,—
    Go ask her, Alice.

THE BALLAD OF "BEAU BROCADE."

"Hark! I hear the sound of coaches!"
—Beggar's Opera.

I.

Seventeen hundred and thirty-nine:—
That was the date of this tale of mine.

First great George was buried and gone;
George the Second was plodding on.

London, then, as the "Guides" aver,
Shared its glories with *Westminster;*

And people of rank, to correct their "tone,"
Went out of town to *Marybone.*

Those were the days of the War with *Spain,*
Porto-Bello would soon be ta'en;

The Ballad of "Beau Brocade."

WHITEFIELD preached to the colliers grim,
Bishops in lawn sleeves preached at him;

WALPOLE talked of "a man and his price";
Nobody's virtue was over-nice :—

Those, in fine, were the brave days when
Coaches were stopped by . . . *Highwaymen!*

And of all the knights of the gentle trade
Nobody bolder than "BEAU BROCADE."

This they knew on the whole way down;
Best,—may be,—at the "*Oak and Crown.*"

(For timorous folk on their pilgrimage
Would "club" for a "Guard" to ride the stage;

And the Guard that rode on more than one
Was the Host of this hostel's sister's son.)

Open we here on a March day fine,
Under the oak with the hanging sign.

There was Barber DICK with his basin by;
Cobbler JOE with the patch on his eye;

The Ballad of "Beau Brocade."

Portly product of Beef and Beer,
JOHN the host, he was standing near.

Straining and creaking, with wheels awry,
Lumbering came the "*Plymouth Fly*";—

Lumbering up from *Bagshot Heath*,
Guard in the basket armed to the teeth;

Passengers heavily armed inside;
Not the less surely the coach had been tried!

Tried!—but a couple of miles away,
By a well-dressed man!—in the open day!

Tried successfully, never a doubt,
Pockets of passengers all turned out!

Cloak-bags rifled, and cushions ripped,—
Even an Ensign's wallet stripped!

Even a Methodist hosier's wife
Offered the choice of her Money or Life!

Highwayman's manners no less polite,
Hoped that their coppers (returned) were right;—

The Ballad of " Beau Brocade."

Sorry to find the company poor,
Hoped next time they 'd travel with more ;—

Plucked them all at his ease, in short :—
Such was the "*Plymouth Fly's*" report.

Sympathy! horror! and wonderment!
" Catch the Villain !"   (But Nobody went.)

Hosier's wife led into the Bar ;—
(That 's where the best strong waters are !)

Followed the tale of the hundred-and-one
Things that Somebody ought to have done.

Ensign (of BRAGG's) made a terrible clangour :
But for the Ladies had drawn his hanger !

Robber, of course, was " BEAU BROCADE ";
Out-spoke DOLLY the Chambermaid.

Devonshire DOLLY, plump and red,
Spoke from the gallery overhead ;—

Spoke it out boldly, staring hard :—
" Why did n't you shoot then, GEORGE the Guard ?"

The Ballad of "Beau Brocade."

Spoke it out bolder, seeing him mute :—
" GEORGE the Guard, why did n't you shoot ?"

Portly JOHN grew pale and red,
(JOHN was afraid of her, people said ;)

Gasped that " DOLLY was surely cracked,"
(JOHN was afraid of her—that 's a fact !)

GEORGE the Guard grew red and pale,
Slowly finished his quart of ale :—

" Shoot ?   Why—Rabbit him !—did n't he shoot ?"
Muttered—"The Baggage was far too 'cute !"

" Shoot ?   Why he 'd flashed the pan in his eye !"
Muttered—"She 'd pay for it by and by !"
Further than this made no reply.

Nor could a further reply be made,
For GEORGE was in league with " BEAU BROCADE "!

And JOHN the Host, in his wakefullest state,
Was not—on the whole—immaculate.

But nobody's virtue was over-nice
When WALPOLE talked of "a man and his price";

And wherever Purity found abode,
'T was certainly *not* on a posting road.

II.

"Forty" followed to "Thirty-nine."
Glorious days of the *Hanover* line!

Princes were born, and drums were banged;
Now and then batches of Highwaymen hanged.

"Glorious news!"—from the *Spanish Main;*
PORTO-BELLO at last was ta'en.

"Glorious news!"—for the liquor trade;
Nobody dreamed of "BEAU BROCADE."

People were thinking of *Spanish Crowns;*
Money was coming from seaport towns!

Nobody dreamed of "BEAU BROCADE,"
(Only DOLLY the Chambermaid!)

Blessings on VERNON! Fill up the cans;
Money was coming in *"Flys"* and *"Vans."*

Possibly, JOHN the Host had heard;
Also, certainly, GEORGE the Guard.

The Ballad of " Beau Brocade."

And DOLLY had possibly tidings, too,
That made her rise from her bed anew,

Plump as ever, but stern of eye,
With a fixed intention to warn the "*Fly*."

Lingering only at JOHN his door,
Just to make sure of a jerky snore;

Saddling the gray mare, *Dumpling Star;*
Fetching the pistol out of the bar;

(The old horse-pistol that, they say,
Came from the battle of *Malplaquet;*)

Loading with powder that maids would use,
Even in " Forty," to clear the flues;

And a couple of silver buttons, the Squire
Gave her, away in *Devonshire*.

These she wadded—for want of better—
With the B—SH—P of L—ND—N's "Pastoral
  Letter";

Looked to the flint, and hung the whole,
Ready to use, at her pocket-hole.

132

The Ballad of "Beau Brocade."

Thus equipped and accoutred, DOLLY
Clattered away to "*Exciseman's Folly*";—

Such was the name of a ruined abode,
Just on the edge of the *London* road.

Thence she thought she might safely try
As soon as she saw it to warn the "*Fly*."

But, as chance fell out, her rein she drew,
As the BEAU came cantering into the view.

By the light of the moon she could see him drest
In his famous gold-sprigged tambour vest;

And under his silver-gray surtout,
The laced, historical coat of blue,

That he wore when he went to *London-Spaw*,
And robbed Sir MUNGO MUCKLETHRAW.

Out-spoke DOLLY the Chambermaid,
(Trembling a little, but not afraid,)
"Stand and Deliver, O 'BEAU BROCADE'!"

But the BEAU drew nearer, and would not speak,
For he saw by the moonlight a rosy cheek;

And a spavined mare that was worth a "cole";
And a girl with her hand at her pocket-hole.

So never a word he spoke as yet,
For he thought 't was a freak of MEG or BET;—
A freak of the "*Rose*" or the "*Rummer*" set.

Out-spoke DOLLY the Chambermaid,
(Tremulous now, and sore afraid,)
"Stand and Deliver, O 'BEAU BROCADE'!"—

Firing then, out of sheer alarm,
Hit the BEAU in the bridle-arm.

Button the first went none knows where,
But it carried away his *solitaire ;*

Button the second a circuit made,
Glanced in under the shoulder-blade ;—
Down from the saddle fell "BEAU BROCADE"!

Down from the saddle and never stirred !—
DOLLY grew white as a *Windsor* curd.

Slipped not less from the mare, and bound
Strips of her kirtle about his wound.

Then, lest his Worship should rise and flee,
Fettered his ankles—tenderly.

Jumped on his chestnut, BET the fleet
(Called after BET of *Portugal Street*);

Came like the wind to the old Inn-door ;—
Roused fat JOHN from a three-fold snore ;—

Vowed she 'd 'peach if he misbehaved . . .
Briefly, the "*Plymouth Fly*" was saved !

Staines and *Windsor* were all on fire :—
DOLLY was wed to a *Yorkshire* squire ;
Went to Town at the K—G's desire !

But whether His M—J—STY saw her or not,
HOGARTH jotted her down on the spot ;

And something of DOLLY one still may trace
In the fresh contours of his "*Milkmaid's*" face.

GEORGE the Guard fled over the sea :
JOHN had a fit—of perplexity ;

Turned King's evidence, sad to state ;—
But JOHN was never immaculate.

The Ballad of "Beau Brocade."

As for the BEAU, he was duly tried,   ·
When his wound was healed, at *Whitsuntide;*

Served—for a day—as the last of "sights,"
To the world of *St. James's-Street* and "*White's*";

Went on his way to TYBURN TREE,
With a pomp befitting his high degree.

Every privilege rank confers:—
Bouquet of pinks at *St. Sepulchre's;*

Flagon of ale at *Holborn Bar;*
Friends (in mourning) to follow his Car—
("t" is omitted where HEROES are!)

Every one knows the speech he made;
Swore that he "rather admired the Jade!"—

Waved to the crowd with his gold-laced hat;
Talked to the Chaplain after that;

Turned to the Topsman undismayed . . .
This was the finish of "BEAU BROCADE"!

———

*And this is the Ballad that seemed to hide
In the leaves of a dusty "*LONDONER'S GUIDE*";*

136

The Ballad of " Beau Brocade."

" *Humbly Inscrib'd*" *(with curls and tails)*
  By the Author to FREDERICK, *Prince of* WALES:—

" *Published by* FRANCIS *and* OLIVER PINE;
  Ludgate-Hill, at the Blackmoor Sign.
  Seventeen-Hundred-and-Thirty-Nine."

POEMS OF THE EIGHTEENTH CENTURY
(FRENCH)

UNE MARQUISE.

A RHYMED MONOLOGUE IN THE LOUVRE.

" Belle Marquise, vos beaux yeux me font mourir d'amour."
—Molière.

I.

As you sit there at your ease,
         O Marquise!
And the men flock round your knees
         Thick as bees,
Mute at every word you utter,
Servants to your least frill flutter,
        " Belle Marquise!"—
As you sit there growing prouder,
  And your ringed hands glance and go,
And your fan's *frou-frou* sounds louder,
  And your *"beaux yeux"* flash and glow;—
Ah, you used them on the Painter,
        As you know,

Une Marquise.

For the Sieur Larose spoke fainter,
   Bowing low,
Thanked Madame and Heaven for Mercy
That each sitter was not Circe,
 Or at least he told you so;—
Growing proud, I say, and prouder
 To the crowd that come and go,
Dainty Deity of Powder,
 Fickle Queen of Fop and Beau,
As you sit where lustres strike you,
   Sure to please,
Do we love you most or like you,
   " Belle Marquise !"

II.

You are fair; O yes, we know it
   Well, Marquise;
For he swore it, your last poet,
   On his knees;
And he called all heaven to witness
Of his ballad and its fitness,
   " Belle Marquise !"—
You were everything in *ère*
(With exception of *sévère*),—
You were *cruelle* and *rebelle*,
With the rest of rhymes as well;

Une Marquise.

You were "*Reine*," and "*Mère d'Amour*";
   You were "*Vénus à Cythère*";
"*Sappho mise en Pompadour*,"
   And "*Minerve en Parabère*";
You had every grace of heaven
   In your most angelic face,
With the nameless finer leaven
   Lent of blood and courtly race;
And he added, too, in duty,
Ninon's wit and Boufflers' beauty;
And La Vallière's *yeux veloutés*
          Followed these;
And you liked it, when he said it
          (On his knees),
And you kept it, and you read it,
     "*Belle Marquise!*"

III.

Yet with us your toilet graces
          Fail to please,
And the last of your last faces,
          And your *mise*;
For we hold you just as real,
     "*Belle Marquise!*"

143

Une Marquise.

As your *Bergers* and *Bergères*,
Iles d'Amour and *Batelières;*
As your *parcs*, and your Versailles,
Gardens, grottoes, and *rocailles;*
As your Naiads and your trees ;—
    Just as near the old ideal
                    Calm and ease,
As the Venus there, by Coustou,
    That a fan would make quite flighty,
Is to her the gods were used to,—
    Is to grand Greek Aphroditè,
                    Sprung from seas.
You are just a porcelain trifle,
            " Belle Marquise!"
Just a thing of puffs and patches,
Made for madrigals and catches,
Not for heart-wounds, but for scratches,
            O Marquise !
Just a pinky porcelain trifle,
            " Belle Marquise!"
Wrought in rarest *rose-Dubarry*,
Quick at verbal point and parry,
Clever, doubtless ;—but to marry,
            No, Marquise !

Une Marquise.

IV.

For your Cupid, you have clipped him,
Rouged and patched him, nipped and snipped
     him,
And with *chapeau-bras* equipped him,
         " Belle Marquise !"
Just to arm you through your wife-time,
And the languors of your life-time,
         " Belle Marquise !"
Say, to trim your toilet tapers,
Or,—to twist your hair in papers,
Or,—to win you from the vapours ;—
         As for these,
You are worth the love they give you,
Till a fairer face outlive you,
  Or a younger grace shall please ;
Till the coming of the crows' feet,
And the backward turn of beaux' feet,
         " Belle Marquise !"—
Till your frothed-out life's commotion
Settles down to Ennui's ocean,
Or a dainty sham devotion,
         " Belle Marquise !"

Une Marquise.

V.

No: we neither like nor love you,
   "*Belle Marquise!*"
Lesser lights we place above you,—
 Milder merits better please.
We have passed from *Philosophe*-dom
 Into plainer modern days,—
Grown contented in our oafdom,
 Giving grace not all the praise;
And, *en partant, Arsinoé,*—
 Without malice whatsoever,—
We shall counsel to our Chloë
 To be rather good than clever;
For we find it hard to smother
 Just one little thought, Marquise!
Wittier perhaps than any other,—
You were neither Wife nor Mother,
   "*Belle Marquise!*"

↓

THE STORY OF ROSINA.

AN INCIDENT IN THE LIFE OF FRANÇOIS BOUCHER.

" On ne badine pas avec l'amour."

THE scene, a wood. A shepherd tip-toe creeping,
   Carries a basket, whence a billet peeps,
To lay beside a silk-clad Oread sleeping
   Under an urn; yet not so sound she sleeps
But that she plainly sees his graceful act;
" He thinks she thinks he thinks she sleeps," in fact.

One hardly needs the "*Peint par François Boucher.*"
   All the sham life comes back again,—one sees
Alcôves, Ruelles, the *Lever,* and the *Coucher,*
   Patches and Ruffles, *Roués* and *Marquises;*
The little great, the infinite small thing
That ruled the hour when Louis Quinze was king.

The Story of Rosina.

For these were yet the days of halcyon weather,—
   A "Martin's summer" when the nation swam,
Aimless and easy as a wayward feather,
   Down the full tide of jest and epigram;—
A careless time, when France's bluest blood
Beat to the tune of "After us the flood."

Plain Roland still was placidly "inspecting,"
   Not now Camille had stirred the Café Foy;
Marat was young, and Guillotin dissecting,
   Corday unborn, and Lamballe in Savoie;
No *faubourg* yet had heard the Tocsin ring:—
This was the summer—when Grasshoppers sing.

And far afield were sun-baked savage creatures,
   Female and male, that tilled the earth, and wrung
Want from the soil;—lean things with livid features,
   Shape of bent man, and voice that never sung:
These were the Ants, for yet to Jacques Bonhomme
Tumbrils were not, nor any sound of drum.

But Boucher was a Grasshopper, and painted,—
   Rose-water Raphael,—*en couleur de rose*,
The crowned Caprice, whose sceptre, nowise sainted,
   Swayed the light realm of ballets and bon-mots;—

The Story of Rosina.

Ruled the dim boudoir's *demi-jour*, or drove
Pink-ribboned flocks through some pink-flowered
    grove.

A laughing Dame, who sailed a laughing cargo
    Of flippant loves along the *Fleuve du Tendre ;*
Whose greatest grace was *jupes à la Camargo,*
    Whose gentlest merit *gentiment se rendre ;*—
Queen of the rouge-cheeked Hours, whose footsteps
    fell
To Rameau's notes, in dances by Gardel;—

Her Boucher served, till Nature's self betraying,
    As Wordsworth sings, the heart that loved her not,
Made of his work a land of languid Maying,
    Filled with false gods and muses misbegot;—
A Versailles Eden of cosmetic youth,
Wherein most things went naked, save the Truth.

Once, only once,—perhaps the last night's revels
    Palled in the after-taste,—our Boucher sighed
For that first beauty, falsely named the Devil's,
    Young-lipped, unlessoned, joyous, and clear-eyed;
Flung down his palette like a weary man,
And sauntered slowly through the Rue Sainte-Anne.

The Story of Rosina.

Wherefore, we know not; but, at times, far nearer
    Things common come, and lineaments half seen
Grow in a moment magically clearer;—
    Perhaps, as he walked, the grass he called "too
        green"
Rose and rebuked him, or the earth "ill-lighted"
Silently smote him with the charms he slighted.

But, as he walked, he tired of god and goddess,
    Nymphs that deny, and shepherds that appeal;
Stale seemed the trick of kerchief and of bodice,
    Folds that confess, and flutters that reveal;
Then as he grew more sad and disenchanted,
Forthwith he spied the very thing he wanted.

So, in the Louvre, the passer-by might spy some
    Arch-looking head, with half-evasive air,
Start from behind the fruitage of Van Huysum,
    Grape-bunch and melon, nectarine and pear:—
Here 't was no Venus of Batavian city,
But a French girl, young, *piquante*, bright, and pretty.

Graceful she was, as some slim marsh-flower shaken
    Among the sallows, in the breezy Spring;
Blithe as the first blithe song of birds that waken,
    Fresh as a fresh young pear-tree blossoming;

The Story of Rosina.

Black was her hair as any blackbird's feather;
Just for her mouth, two rose-buds grew together.

Sloes were her eyes; but her soft cheeks were peaches,
   Hued like an Autumn pippin, where the red
Seems to have burned right through the skin, and
     reaches
   E'en to the core; and if you spoke, it spread
Up till the blush had vanquished all the brown,
And like two birds, the sudden lids dropped down.

As Boucher smiled, the bright black eyes ceased
    dancing,
   As Boucher spoke, the dainty red eclipse
Filled all the face from cheek to brow, enhancing
   Half a shy smile that dawned around the lips.
Then a shrill mother rose upon the view;
" *Cerises, M'sieu? Rosine, dépêchez-vous!*"

Deep in the fruit her hands Rosina buries,
   Soon in the scale the ruby bunches lay.
The painter, watching the suspended cherries,
   Never had seen such little fingers play;—
As for the arm, no Hebè's could be rounder;
Low in his heart a whisper said "I 've found her."

The Story of Rosina.

"Woo first the mother, if you 'd win the daughter!"
    Boucher was charmed, and turned to *Madame*
        Mère,
Almost with tears of suppliance besought her
    Leave to immortalize a face so fair;
Praised and cajoled so craftily that straightway
Voici Rosina,—standing at his gateway.

Shy at the first, in time Rosina's laughter
    Rang through the studio as the girlish face
Peeped from some painter's travesty, or after
    Showed like an Omphale in lion's case;
Gay as a thrush, that from the morning dew
Pipes to the light its clear "*Réveillez-vous.*"

Just a mere child with sudden ebullitions,
    Flashes of fun, and little bursts of song,
Petulant pains, and fleeting pale contritions,
    Mute little moods of misery and wrong;
Only a child, of Nature's rarest making,
Wistful and sweet,—and with a heart for breaking!

Day after day the little loving creature
    Came and returned; and still the Painter felt,
Day after day, the old theatric Nature
    Fade from his sight, and like a shadow melt,—

The Story of Rosina.

Paniers and Powder, Pastoral and Scene,
Killed by the simple beauty of Rosine.

As for the girl, she turned to her new being,—
  Came, as a bird that hears its fellow call;
Blessed, as the blind that blesses God for seeing;
  Grew, as a flower on which the sun-rays fall;
Loved if you will;—she never named it so:
Love comes unseen,—we only see it go.

There is a figure among Boucher's sketches,
  Slim,—a child-face, the eyes as black as beads,
Head set askance, and hand that shyly stretches
  Flowers to the passer, with a look that pleads.
This was no other than Rosina surely;—
None else that Boucher knew could look so purely.

But forth her Story, for I will not tarry,
  Whether he loved the little "nut-brown maid";
If, of a truth, he counted this to carry
  Straight to the end, or just the whim obeyed,
Nothing we know, but only that before
More had been done, a finger tapped the door.

Opened Rosina to the unknown comer.
  'T was a young girl—"*une pauvre fille*," she said,

The Story of Rosina.

"They had been growing poorer all the summer;
    Father was lame, and mother lately dead;
Bread was so dear, and,—oh! but want was bitter,
    Would Monsieur pay to have her for a sitter?

Men called her pretty."   Boucher looked a minute:
    Yes, she was pretty; and her face beside
Shamed her poor clothing by a something in it,—
    Grace, and a presence hard to be denied;
This was no common offer it was certain;—
"*Allez*, Rosina! sit behind the curtain."

Meantime the Painter, with a mixed emotion,
    Drew and re-drew his ill-disguised Marquise,
Passed in due time from praises to devotion;
    Last when his sitter left him on his knees,
Rose in a maze of passion and surprise,—
Rose, and beheld Rosina's saddened eyes.

Thrice-happy France, whose facile sons inherit
    Still in the old traditionary way,
Power to enjoy—with yet a rarer merit,
    Power to forget! Our Boucher rose, I say,
With hand still prest to heart, with pulses throbbing,
And blankly stared at poor Rosina sobbing.

The Story of Rosina.

"This was no model, *M'sieu*, but a lady."
    Boucher was silent, for he knew it true. .
"*Est-ce que vous l'aimez?*"   Never answer made he!
    Ah, for the old love fighting with the new!
"*Est-ce que vous l'aimez?*" sobbed Rosina's sorrow.
"*Bon!*" murmured Boucher; "she will come to-mor-
      row."

How like a Hunter thou, O Time, dost harry
    Us, thine oppressed, and pleasured with the chase
Sparest to strike thy sorely-running quarry,
    Following not less with unrelenting face.
Time, if Love hunt, and Sorrow hunt, with thee,
Woe to the Fawn! There is no way to flee.

Woe to Rosina! By To-morrow stricken,
    Swift from her life the sun of gold declined.
Nothing remained but those gray shades that thicken,
    Cloud and the cold,—the loneliness—the wind.
Only a little by the door she lingers,—
Waits, with wrung lip and interwoven fingers.

No, not a sign. Already with the Painter
    Grace and the nymphs began recovered reign;
Truth was no more, and Nature, waxing fainter,
    Paled to the old sick Artifice again.

155.

The Story of Rosina.

Seeing Rosina going out to die,
How should he know what Fame had passed him by?

Going to die! For who shall waste in sadness,
   Shorn of the sun, the very warmth and light,
Miss the green welcome of the sweet earth's gladness,
   Lose the round life that only Love makes bright:
There is no succour if these things are taken.
None but Death loves the lips by Love forsaken.

So, in a little, when those Two had parted,—
   Tired of himself, and weary as before,
Boucher remembering, sick and sorry-hearted,
   Stayed for a moment by Rosina's door.
" Ah, the poor child!" the neighbour's cry of her,
" *Morte, M'sieu, morte! On dit,—de peines du cœur!*"

Just for a second, say, the tidings shocked him,
   Say, in his eye a sudden tear-drop shone,—
Just for a second a dull feeling mocked him
   With a vague sense of something priceless gone;
Then,—for at best 't was but the empty type,
The husk of man with which the days were ripe,—

Then, he forgot her. But, for you that slew her,
   You, her own sister, that with airy ease,

The Story of Rosina.

Just for a moment's fancy could undo her,
    Pass on your way.   A little while, Marquise,
Be the sky silent, be the sea serene;
A pleasant passage—*à Sainte Guillotine.*

As for Rosina,—for the quiet sleeper,
    Whether stone hides her, or the happy grass,
If the sun quickens, if the dews beweep her,
    Laid in the Madeleine or Montparnasse,
Nothing we know,—but that her heart is cold,
Poor beating heart!   And so the story 's told.

A REVOLUTIONARY RELIC.

OLD it is, and worn and battered,
  As I lift it from the stall;
And the leaves are frayed and tattered,
And the pendent sides are shattered,
  Pierced and blackened by a ball.

'T is the tale of grief and gladness
  Told by sad St. Pierre of yore,
That in front of France's madness
Hangs a strange seductive sadness,
  Grown pathetic evermore.

And a perfume round it hovers,
  Which the pages half reveal,
For a folded corner covers,
Interlaced, two names of lovers,—
  A "Savignac" and "Lucile."

158

A Revolutionary Relic.

As I read I marvel whether,
   In some pleasant old château,
Once they read this book together,
In the scented summer weather,
   With the shining Loire below.

Nooked—secluded from espial,
   Did Love slip and snare them so,
While the hours danced round the dial
To the sound of flute and viol,
   In that pleasant old château?

Did it happen that no single
   Word of mouth could either speak?
Did the brown and gold hair mingle,
Did the shamed skin thrill and tingle
   To the shock of cheek and cheek?

Did they feel with that first flushing
   Some new sudden power to feel,
Some new inner spring set gushing
At the names together rushing
   Of "Savignac" and "Lucile"?

Did he drop on knee before her—
   " *Son Amour, son Cœur, sa Reine*"—

A Revolutionary Relic.

In his high-flown way adore her,
Urgent, eloquent implore her,
   Plead his pleasure and his pain?

Did she turn with sight swift-dimming,
   And the quivering lip we know,
With the full, slow eyelid brimming,
With the languorous pupil swimming,
   Like the love of Mirabeau?

Stretch her hand from cloudy frilling,
   For his eager lips to press;
In a flash all fate fulfilling
Did he catch her, trembling, thrilling—
   Crushing life to one caress?

Did they sit in that dim sweetness
   Of attained love's after-calm,
Marking not the world—its meetness,
Marking Time not, nor his fleetness,
   Only happy, palm to palm?

Till at last she,—sunlight smiting
   Red on wrist and cheek and hair,—
Sought the page where love first lighting,

A Revolutionary Relic.

Fixed their fate, and, in this writing,
   Fixed the record of it there.

   .   .   .   .   .

Did they marry midst the smother,
   Shame and slaughter of it all ?
Did she wander like that other
Woful, wistful, wife and mother,
   Round and round his prison wall ;—

Wander wailing, as the plover
   Waileth, wheeleth, desolate,
Heedless of the hawk above her,
While as yet the rushes cover,
   Waning fast, her wounded mate ;—

Wander, till his love's eyes met hers,
   Fixed and wide in their despair ?
Did he burst his prison fetters,
Did he write sweet, yearning letters,
   " *A Lucile,—en Angleterre*" ?

Letters where the reader, reading,
   Halts him with a sudden stop,
For he feels a man's heart bleeding,
Draining out its pain's exceeding—
   Half a life, at every drop :

A Revolutionary Relic.

Letters where Love's iteration
  Seems to warble and to rave;
Letters where the pent sensation
Leaps to lyric exultation,
  Like a song-bird from a grave.

Where, through Passion's wild repeating,
  Peep the Pagan and the Gaul,
Politics and love competing,
Abelard and Cato greeting,
  Rousseau ramping over all.

Yet your critic's right—you waive it,
  Whirled along the fever-flood;
And its touch of truth shall save it,
And its tender rain shall lave it,
For at least you read *Amavit*,
  Written there in tears of blood.

.   .   .   .

Did they hunt him to his hiding,
  Tracking traces in the snow?
Did they tempt him out, confiding,
Shoot him ruthless down, deriding,
  By the ruined old château?

A Revolutionary Relic.

Left to lie, with thin lips resting
　　Frozen to a smile of scorn,
Just the bitter thought's suggesting,
At this excellent new jesting
　　Of the rabble Devil-born.

Till some "tiger-monkey," finding
　　These few words the covers bear,
Some swift rush of pity blinding,
Sent them in the shot-pierced binding
　　"*A Lucile, en Angleterre.*"

　·　　·　　·　　·　　·　　·

Fancies only!　Nought the covers,
　　Nothing more the leaves reveal,
Yet I love it for its lovers,
For the dream that round it hovers
　　Of "Savignac" and "Lucile."

163

PROVERBS IN PORCELAIN

PROLOGUE.

Assume *that we are friends.   Assume*
A common taste for old costume,
  Old pictures,—books.   Then dream us sitting,—
Us two,—in some soft-lighted room.

Outside the wind ;—the "ways are mire."
We, with our faces towards the fire,
  Finished the feast not full but fitting,
Watch the light-leaping flames aspire.

Silent at first, in time we glow ;
Discuss "eclectics," high and low ;
  Inspect engravings, 'twixt us passing
The fancies of Detroy, Moreau ;

" Reveils " and " Couchers," " Balls " and " Fêtes ";
  Anon we glide to " crocks " and plates,
    Grow eloquent on glaze and classing,
  And half-pathetic over " states."

167

Prologue.

Then *I produce my Prize, in truth ;—*
Six groups in SÈVRES, *fresh as Youth,*
   And rare as Love.   You pause, you wonder,
(Pretend to doubt the marks, forsooth!)

And so we fall to why and how
The fragile figures smile and bow ;
   Divine, at length, the fable under . . . .
Thus grew the " Scenes" that follow now.

THE BALLAD À-LA-MODE.

" Tout vient à point à qui peut attendre."

SCENE.—*A Boudoir Louis-Quinze, painted with Cupids*
shooting at Butterflies.

THE COUNTESS.   THE BARON *(her cousin and suitor).*

THE COUNTESS *(looking up from her work).*
Baron, you doze.

THE BARON *(closing his book).*
I, Madame ?   No.
I wait your order—Stay or Go.

THE COUNTESS.
Which means, I think, that Go or Stay
Affects you nothing, either way.

169

The Ballad à-la-Mode.

THE BARON.

Excuse me,—By your favour graced
My inclinations are effaced.

THE COUNTESS.

Or much the same.   How keen you grow!
You must be reading MARIVAUX.

THE BARON.

Nay,—'t was a song of SAINTE-AULAIRE.

THE COUNTESS.

Then read me one.   We 've time to spare:
If I can catch the clock-face there,
'T is barely eight.

THE BARON.

                    What shall it be,—
A tale of woe, or perfidy?

THE COUNTESS.

Not woes, I beg.   I doubt your woes:
But perfidy, of course, one knows.

THE BARON *(reads).*
" Ah, Phillis! cruel Phillis!
(I heard a Shepherd say,)

The Ballad à-la-Mode.

You hold me with your Eyes, and yet
You bid me—Go my way !

" Ah, Colin ! foolish Colin !
(The Maiden answered so,)
If that be All, the Ill is small,
I close them— You may go !

" But when her Eyes she opened,
(Although the Sun it shone,)
She found the Shepherd had not stirred—
' Because the Light was gone !'

" Ah, Cupid ! wanton Cupid !
'T was ever thus your way :
When Maids would bid you ply your Wings,
You find Excuse to stay !"

THE COUNTESS.
Famous!   He earned whate'er he got:—
But there 's some sequel, is there not ?

THE BARON *(turning the page).*
I think not.—No.   Unless 't is this:
My fate is far more hard than his;—.
In fact, *your* Eyes—

The Ballad à-la-Mode.

THE COUNTESS.
      Now, that 's a breach !
Your bond is—not to make a speech.
And we must start—so call JUSTINE.
I know exactly what you mean !—
Give me your arm—

THE BARON.
      If, in return,
Countess, I could your hand but earn !

THE COUNTESS.
I thought as much.   This comes, you see,
Of sentiment, and Arcady,
Where vows are hung on every tree . . .

THE BARON *(offering his arm, with a low bow)*.
And no one dreams—of PERFIDY.

THE METAMORPHOSIS.

" On s'enrichit quand on dort."

SCENE.—*A high stone Seat in an Alley of clipped Lime-trees.*

THE ABBÉ TIRILI.   MONSIEUR L'ÉTOILE.

THE ABBÉ *(writing).*

" This shepherdess Dorine adored—"
What rhyme is next?   *Implored?—ignored?*
Poured?—soared?—afford?   That facile dunce,
L'ÉTOILE, would cap the line at once.
'T will come in time.   Meanwhile, suppose
We take a meditative doze.
   (Sleeps.   By-and-by his paper falls.)

   M. L'ÉTOILE *(approaching from the back).*
Some one before me.   What! 't is you,
Monsieur the Scholar?   Sleeping too!

173

The Metamorphosis.

(Picks up the fluttering paper.)
More " *Tales,*" of course.   One can't refuse
To chase so fugitive a Muse !
Verses are public, too, that fly
" *Cum privilegio* "—*Zephyri !*
                    (Reads.)
" CLITANDER AND DORINE."   Insane !
He fancies he 's a LA FONTAINE !
" *In early days, the Gods, we find,*
   Paid frequent Visits to Mankind ;—
   At least, authentic Records say so
   In Publius Ovidius Naso."
(Three names for one.   This passes all.
'T is " furiously " classical !)
" *No doubt their Purpose oft would be*
   Some ' Nodus dignus Vindice';
   ' On dit,' not less, these earthly Tours
   Were mostly matters of Amours.
   And woe to him whose luckless Flame
   Impeded that Olympic Game ;
   Ere he could say an ' Ave' o'er,
   They changed him—like a Louis-d'or."
(" *Aves,*" and current coinage !   O !—
O shade of NICHOLAS BOILEAU !)

The Metamorphosis.

" *Bird, Beast, or River he became :*
 With Women it was much the same.
 In Ovid Case to Case succeeds ;
 But Names the Reader never reads."
 (That is, Monsieur the Abbé feels
 His quantities are out at heels !)
" *Suffices that, for this our Tale,*
 There dwelt in a Thessalian Vale,
 Of Tales like this the constant Scene,
 A Shepherdess, by name Dorine.
 Trim Waist, ripe Lips, bright Eyes, had she ;—
 In short, the whole Artillery.
 Her Beauty made some local Stir ;—
 Men marked it.   So did Jupiter.
 This Shepherdess Dorine adored . . ."
 Implored, ignored, and *soared,* and *poured—*
 (He 's scrawled them here !)   We 'll sum in brief
 His fable on his second leaf.
                    (Writes.)
 There, they shall know who 't was that wrote :—
 " L'ÉTOILE'S *is but a mock-bird's note.*"   [*Exit.*

          THE ABBÉ *(waking).*
 Implored 's the word, I think.   But where,—
 Where is my paper ?   Ah ! 't is there !
 Eh ! what ?

175

The Metamorphosis.

(Reads.)

. The Metamorphosis.

(not in Ovid.)

" *The Shepherdess Dorine adored*
The Shepherd-Boy Clitander;
But Jove himself, Olympus' Lord,
The Shepherdess Dorine adored.
Our Abbé's Aid the Pair Implored;—
  And changed to Goose and Gander,
The Shepherdess Dorine adored
  The Shepherd-Boy Clitander!"

L'Étoile,—by all the Muses!

Peste!

He 's off, post-haste, to tell the rest.
No matter.   Laugh, Sir Dunce, to-day;
Next time 't will be *my* turn to play.

THE SONG OUT OF SEASON.

"Point de culte sans mystère."

SCENE.—*A Corridor in a Château, with Busts and Venice chandeliers.*

MONSIEUR L'ÉTOILE.   TWO VOICES.

M. L'ÉTOILE *(carrying a Rose)*.
This is the place.   MUTINE said here.
" Through the Mancini room, and near
The fifth Venetian chandelier . . ."
The fifth ?—She knew there were but four;—
Still, here 's the *busto* of the Moor.
(Humming.)
Tra-la, tra-la ! If BIJOU wake,
She 'll bark, no doubt, and spoil my shake!
I 'll tap, I think.   One can't mistake;
    This surely is the door.

The Song Out of Season.

(Sings softly.)
" *When Jove, the Skies' Director,*
First saw you sleep of yore,
He cried aloud for Nectar,
' *The Nectar quickly pour,—*
The Nectar, Hebe, pour! ' "

(No sound.   I 'll tap once more.)

(Sings again.)
" *Then came the Sire Apollo,*
He past you where you lay;
' *Come, Dian, rise and follow*
The dappled Hart to slay,—
The rapid Hart to slay.' "

(A rustling within.)
(Coquette!   She heard before.)

(Sings again.)
" *And urchin Cupid after*
Beside the Pillow curled,
He whispered you with Laughter,
' *Awake and witch the World,—*
O Venus, witch the World! ' "

(Now comes the last.   'T is scarcely worse,
I think, than Monsieur l'ABBÉ's verse.)

The Song Out of Season.

" *So waken, waken, waken,*
O You, whom we adore !
Where Gods can be mistaken,
Mere Mortals must be more,—
*Poor Mortals must be more ! *"

(That merits an *encore !)*

" *So waken, waken, waken !*
O you *whom we adore ! *"

(An energetic Voice.*)*
'T is thou, Antoine?   Ah Addle-pate !
Ah Thief of Valet, always late !
Have I not told thee half-past eight
A thousand times !
(Great agitation.)
But wait,—but wait,—

M. L'Étoile *(stupefied).*
Just Skies !   What hideous roar !—
What lungs !   The infamous Soubrette !
This is a turn I sha'n't forget :—
To make me sing my *chansonnette*
Before old Jourdain's door !

The Song Out of Season.

(Retiring slowly.)
And yet, and yet,—it can't be she.
They prompted her.   Who can it be?

(A second VOICE.*)*
IT WAS THE ABBÉ TI—RI—LI!
(In a mocking falsetto.)
" *Where Gods can be mistaken,*
Mere Poets must be more,—
BAD POETS *must be more!*"

180

THE CAP THAT FITS.

" Qui sème épines n'aille déchaux."

SCENE.—*A Salon with blue and white Panels.   Outside, Persons pass and re-pass upon a Terrace.*

HORTENSE.   ARMANDE.   MONSIEUR LOYAL.

HORTENSE *(behind her fan).*
Not young, I think.

ARMANDE *(raising her eye-glass).*
                         And faded, too!—
Quite faded!   Monsieur, what say you?

M. LOYAL.
Nay, I defer to you.   In truth,
To me she seems all grace and youth.

The Cap that Fits.

HORTENSE.

Graceful ?   You think it ?   What, with hands
That hang like this *(with a gesture).*

ARMANDE.

And how she stands!

M. LOYAL.

Nay, I am wrong again.   I thought
Her air delightfully untaught!

HORTENSE.

But you amuse me—

M. LOYAL.

Still her dress,—
Her dress at least, you *must* confess—

ARMANDE.

Is odious simply!   JACOTOT
Did not supply that lace, I know;
And where, I ask, has mortal seen
A hat unfeathered!

HORTENSE.

Edged with green!

182

The Cap that Fits.

M. LOYAL.

The word reminds me.   Let me say
A Fable that I heard to-day.
Have I permission?

BOTH *(with enthusiasm)*.
                              Monsieur, pray!

M. LOYAL.

" *Myrtilla (lest a Scandal rise*
  The Lady's Name I thus disguise),
  Dying of Ennui, once decided,—
  Much on Resource herself she prided,—
  To choose a Hat.   Forthwith she flies
  On that momentous Enterprise.
  Whether to Petit or Legros,
  I know not: only this I know ;—
  Head-dresses then, of any Fashion,
  Bore Names of Quality or Passion.
  Myrtilla tried them, almost all :
  ' Prudence,' she felt, was somewhat small ;
  ' Retirement' seemed the Eyes to hide ;
  ' Content,' at once, she cast aside.
  ' Simplicity,'—'t was out of place ;
  ' Devotion,' for an older face ;

The Cap that Fits.

Briefly, Selection smaller grew,
' Vexatious ! odious !'—none would do !
Then, on a sudden, she espied
One that she thought she had not tried :
Becoming, rather,—' edged with green,'—
Roses in yellow, Thorns between.
' Quick ! Bring me that !' 'T is brought.
    ' Complete,
Divine, Enchanting, Tasteful, Neat,'
In all the Tones. ' And this you call—?'
'"ILL-NATURE," Madame. It fits all.'"

HORTENSE.
A thousand thanks! So naively turned!

ARMANDE.
So useful too,—to those concerned!
'T is yours?

M. LOYAL.
    Ah no,—some cynic wit's;
And called (I think)—
    (Placing his hat upon his breast),
        "The Cap that Fits."

THE SECRETS OF THE HEART.

" Le cœur mène où il va."

SCENE.—*A Chalet covered with Honeysuckle.*

NINETTE.   NINON.

NINETTE.

This way—

NINON.

No, this way—

NINETTE.

This way, then.
(They enter the Chalet.)
You are as changing, Child,—as Men.

NINON.

But are they ?   Is it true, I mean ?
Who said it ?

NINETTE.
Sister SÉRAPHINE.
She was so pious and so good,
With such sad eyes beneath her hood,
And such poor little feet,—all bare !
Her name was EUGÉNIE LA FÈRE.
She used to tell us,—moonlight nights,—
When I was at the Carmelites.

NINON.
Ah, then it must be right.   And yet,
Suppose for once—suppose, NINETTE—

NINETTE.
But what ?—

NINON.
Suppose it were not so ?
Suppose there *were* true men, you know !

NINETTE.
And then ?

NINON.
Why,—if that could occur,
What kind of man should you prefe-

186

NINETTE.

What looks, you mean?

NINON.

      Looks, voice and all.

NINETTE.

Well, as to that, he must be tall,
Or say, not " tall,"—of middle size;
And next, he must have laughing eyes,
And a hook-nose,—with, underneath,
O! what a row of sparkling teeth !—

NINON *(touching her cheek suspiciously)*.
Has he a scar on this side?

NINETTE.

             Hush !

Someone is coming.   No; a thrush:
I see it swinging there.

NINON.

      Go on.

NINETTE.

Then he must fence, (ah, look, 't is gone !)
And dance like Monseigneur, and sing

" Love was a Shepherd " :—everything
    That men do.   Tell me yours, NINON.

NINON.

Shall I ?   Then mine has black, black hair,
I mean he *should* have ; then an air
Half sad, half noble ; features thin ;
A little *royale* on the chin ;
And such a pale, high brow.   And then,
He is a prince of gentlemen ;—
He, too, can ride and fence, and write
Sonnets and madrigals, yet fight
No worse for that—

NINETTE.

        I know your man.

NINON.

And I know yours.   But you 'll not tell,—
Swear it !

NINETTE.

    I swear upon this fan,—
My Grandmother's !

NINON.

        And I, I swear
On this old turquoise *reliquaire,*—

The Secrets of the Heart.

My great,—*great* Grandmother's ! !—
(*After a pause.*)

NINETTE !

I feel *so* sad.

NINETTE.
I too.   But why ?

NINON.
Alas, I know not !

NINETTE *(with a sigh).*
Nor do I.

189

"GOOD-NIGHT, BABETTE!"

" Si vieillesse pouvait !—"

SCENE.—*A small neat Room. In a high Voltaire Chair
sits a white-haired old Gentleman.*

MONSIEUR VIEUXBOIS.   BABETTF..

M. VIEUXBOIS *(turning querulously)*.
Day of my life! Where *can* she get?
BABETTE! I say! BABETTE!—BABETTE!!

BABETTE *(entering hurriedly)*.
Coming, M'sieu'! If M'sieu' speaks
So loud he won't be well for weeks!

M. VIEUXBOIS.
Where have you been?

BABETTE.
Why M'sieu' knows :—
April!...Ville-d'Avray!...Ma'am'selle ROSE!

190

" *Good-night, Babette !*"

M. VIEUXBOIS.

Ah! I am old,—and I forget.
Was the place growing green, BABETTE ?

BABETTE.

But of a greenness !—yes, M'sieu' !
And then the sky so blue !—so blue !
And when I dropped my *immortelle*,
How the birds sang !
    (Lifting her apron to her eyes.)
          This poor Ma'am'selle !

M. VIEUXBOIS.

You 're a good girl, BABETTE, but she,—
She was an Angel, verily.
Sometimes I think I see her yet
Stand smiling by the cabinet;
And once, I know, she peeped and laughed
Betwixt the curtains . . .
          Where 's the draught ?
    (She gives him a cup.)
Now I shall sleep, I think, BABETTE ;—
Sing me your Norman *chansonnette*.

BABETTE *(sings).*
" *Once at the Angelus*
    (Ere I was dead),

"Good-night, Babette!"

Angels all glorious
    Came to my Bed ;—
Angels in blue and white
    Crowned on the Head."

M. VIEUXBOIS *(drowsily).*
"She was an Angel"..."Once she laughed"...
What, was I dreaming?
                Where 's the draught?

BABETTE *(showing the empty cup).*
The draught, M'sieu' ?

M. VIEUXBOIS.
             How I forget !
I am so old ! But sing, BABETTE !

BABETTE *(sings).*
" One was the Friend I left
    Stark in the Snow ;
One was the Wife that died
    Long,—long ago ;
One was the Love I lost . . .
    How could she know ? "

M. VIEUXBOIS *(murmuring).*
Ah, PAUL !...old PAUL !...EULALIE too !
And ROSE...And O ! "the sky so blue !"

" Good-night, Babette !"

BABETTE *(sings).*
" One had my Mother's eyes,
Wistful and mild ;
One had my Father's face ;
One was a Child :
All of them bent to me,—
Bent down and smiled !"

(He is asleep !)

M. VIEUXBOIS *(almost inaudibly).*
"How I forget !"
"I am so old !"..."Good-night, BABETTE !"

EPILOGUE.

Heigho! how chill the evenings get!
Good-night, NINON!—*good-night,* NINETTE!
   Your little Play is played and finished;—
Go back, then, to your Cabinet!

LOYAL, L'ÉTOILE! *no more to-day!*
Alas! they heed not what we say:
   They smile with ardour undiminished;
But we,—we are not always gay!

MISCELLANEOUS POEMS

A SONG OF THE FOUR SEASONS.

WHEN Spring comes laughing
  By vale and hill,
By wind-flower walking
  And daffodil,—
Sing stars of morning,
  Sing morning skies,
Sing blue of speedwell,
  And my Love's eyes.

When comes the Summer,
  Full-leaved and strong,
And gay birds gossip
  The orchard long,—
Sing hid, sweet honey
  That no bee sips;
Sing red, red roses,
  And my Love's lips.

A Song of the Four Seasons.

When Autumn scatters
　　The leaves again,
And piled sheaves bury
　　The broad-wheeled wain,—
Sing flutes of harvest
　　Where men rejoice;
Sing rounds of reapers,
　　And my Love's voice.

But when comes Winter
　　With hail and storm,
And red fire roaring
　　And ingle warm,—
Sing first sad going
　　Of friends that part;
Then sing glad meeting
　　And my Love's heart.

THE PARADOX OF TIME.

(A VARIATION ON RONSARD.)

" *Le temps s'en va, le temps s'en va, ma dame!*
Las! le temps non: mais NOUS *nous en allons!* "

TIME goes, you say? Ah no!
Alas, Time stays, *we* go;
   Or else, were this not so,
What need to chain the hours,
For Youth were always ours?
   Time goes, you say?—ah no!

Ours is the eyes' deceit
Of men whose flying feet
   Lead through some landscape low;
We pass, and think we see
The earth's fixed surface flee :—
   Alas, Time stays,—we go!

The Paradox of Time.

Once in the days of old,
Your locks were curling gold,
  And mine had shamed the crow;
Now, in the self-same stage,
We 've reached the silver age;
  Time goes, you say?—ah no!

Once, when my voice was strong,
I filled the woods with song
  To praise your "rose" and "snow";
My bird, that sang, is dead;
Where are your roses fled?
  Alas, Time stays,—we go!

See, in what traversed ways,
What backward Fate delays
  The hopes we used to know;
Where are our old desires?—
Ah, where those vanished fires?
  Time goes, you say?—ah no!

How far, how far, O Sweet,
The past behind our feet
  Lies in the even-glow!
Now, on the forward way,
Let us fold our hands and pray;
  Alas, Time stays,—*we* go!

TO A GREEK GIRL.

(AFTER A WEEK OF LANDOR'S "HELLENICS.")

WITH breath of thyme and bees that hum,
Across the years you seem to come,—
Across the years with nymph-like head,
And wind-blown brows unfilleted;
A girlish shape that slips the bud
  , In lines of unspoiled symmetry;
A girlish shape that stirs the blood
   With pulse of Spring, Autonoë!

Where'er you pass,—where'er you go,
I hear the pebbly rillet flow;
Where'er you go,—where'er you pass,
There comes a gladness on the grass;
You bring blithe airs where'er you tread,—
   Blithe airs that blow from down and sea;
You wake in me a Pan not dead,—
   Not wholly dead!—Autonoë!

To a Greek Girl.

How sweet with you on some green sod
To wreathe the rustic garden-god;
How sweet beneath the chestnut's shade
With you to weave a basket-braid;
To watch across the stricken chords
   Your rosy-twinkling fingers flee;
Or woo you in soft woodland words,
   With woodland pipe, Autonoë!

In vain,—in vain!   The years divide:
Where Thamis rolls a murky tide,
I sit and fill my painful reams,
And see you only in my dreams;—
A vision, like Alcestis, brought
   From under-lands of Memory,—
A dream of Form in days of Thought,—
   A dream,—a dream, Autonoë!

THE DEATH OF PROCRIS.

A VERSION SUGGESTED BY THE SO-NAMED PICTURE OF
PIERO DI COSIMO, IN THE NATIONAL GALLERY.

PROCRIS, the nymph, had wedded Cephalus;—
He, till the spring had warmed to slow-winged days
Heavy with June, untired and amorous,
Named her his love; but now, in unknown ways,
His heart was gone; and evermore his gaze
Turned from her own, and ever farther ranged
His woodland war; while she, in dull amaze,
Beholding with the hours her husband changed,
Sighed for his lost caress, by some hard god estranged.

So, on a day, she rose and found him not.
Alone, with wet, sad eye, she watched the shade
Brighten below a soft-rayed sun that shot
Arrows of light through all the deep-leaved glade;
Then, with weak hands, she knotted up the braid

The Death of Procris.

Of her brown hair, and o'er her shoulders cast
Her crimson weed; with faltering fingers made
Her golden girdle's clasp to join, and past
Down to the trackless wood, full pale and overcast.

And all day long her slight spear devious flew,
And harmless swerved her arrows from their aim,
For ever, as the ivory bow she drew,
Before her ran the still unwounded game.
Then, at the last, a hunter's cry there came,
And, lo, a hart that panted with the chase,
Thereat her cheek was lightened as with flame,
And swift she gat her to a leafy place,
Thinking, "I yet may chance unseen to see his face."

Leaping he went, this hunter Cephalus,
Bent in his hand his cornel bow he bare,
Supple he was, round-limbed and vigorous,
Fleet as his dogs, a lean Laconian pair.
He, when he spied the brown of Procris' hair
Move in the covert, deeming that apart
Some fawn lay hidden, loosed an arrow there;
Nor cared to turn and seek the speeded dart,
Bounding above the fern, fast following up the hart.

But Procris lay among the white wind-flowers,
Shot in the throat.   From out the little wound

The Death of Procris.

The slow blood drained, as drops in autumn showers
Drip from the leaves upon the sodden ground.
None saw her die but Lelaps, the swift hound,
That watched her dumbly with a wistful fear,
Till, at the dawn, the hornèd wood-men found
And bore her gently on a sylvan bier,
To lie beside the sea,—with many an uncouth tear.

205

THE PRAYER OF THE SWINE TO CIRCE.

Huddling they came, with shag sides caked of
    mire,—
With hoofs fresh sullied from the troughs o'er-
    turned,—
With wrinkling snouts,—yet eyes in which desire
Of some strange thing unutterably burned,
Unquenchable; and still where'er She turned
They rose about her, striving each o'er each,
With restless, fierce impórtuning that yearned
Through those brute masks some piteous tale to
    teach,
Yet lacked the words thereto, denied the power of
    speech.

For these—Eurylochus alone escaping—
In truth, that small exploring band had been,
Whom wise Odysseus, dim precaution shaping,
Ever at heart, of peril unforeseen,
Had sent inland;—whom then the islet-Queen,—

The Prayer of the Swine to Circe.

The fair disastrous daughter of the Sun,—
Had turned to likeness of the beast unclean,
With evil wand transforming one by one
To shapes of loathly swine, imbruted and undone.

But "the men's minds remained," and these for ever
Made hungry suppliance through the fire-red eyes;
Still searching aye, with impotent endeavour,
To find, if yet, in any look, there lies
A saving hope, or if they might surprise
In that cold face soft pity's spark concealed,
Which she, still scorning, evermore denies;
Nor was there in her any ruth revealed
To whom with such mute speech and dumb words they
        appealed.

What hope is ours—what hope! To find no mercy
After much war, and many travails done?—
Ah, kinder far than thy fell philtres, Circe,
The ravening Cyclops and the Læstrigon!
And O, thrice cursèd be Laertes' son,
By whom, at last, we watch the days decline
With no fair ending of the quest begun,
Condemned in styes to weary and to pine
And with men's hearts to beat through this foul front of
        swine!

The Prayer of the Swine to Circe.

For us not now,—for us, alas ! no more
The old green glamour of the glancing sea ;
For us not now the laughter of the oar,—
The strong-ribbed keel wherein our comrades be ;
Not now, at even, any more shall we,
By low-browed banks and reedy river places,
Watch the beast hurry and the wild fowl flee ;
Or steering shoreward, in the upland spaces
Have sight of curling smoke and fair-skinned foreign
      faces.

Alas for us !—for whom the columned houses
We left afore-time, cheerless must abide ;
Cheerless the hearth where now no guest carouses,—
No minstrel raises song at eventide ;
And O, more cheerless than aught else beside,
The wistful hearts with heavy longing full ;—
The wife that watched us on the waning tide,—
The sire whose eyes with weariness are dull,—
The mother whose slow tears fall on the carded wool.

If swine we be,—if we indeed be swine,
Daughter of Persé, make us swine indeed,
Well-pleased on litter-straw to lie supine,—
Well-pleased on mast and acorn-shales to feed,
Stirred by all instincts of the bestial breed ;

The Prayer of the Swine to Circe.

But O Unmerciful !   O Pitiless !
Leave us not thus with sick men's hearts to bleed !—
To waste long days in yearning, dumb distress
And memory of things gone, and utter hopelessness !

Leave us at least, if not the things we were,   ·
At least consentient to the thing we be ;
Not hapless doomed to loathe the forms we bear,
And senseful roll in senseless savagery ;
For surely cursed above all cursed are we,
And surely this the bitterest of ill ;—
To feel the old aspirings fair and free,
Become blind motions of a powerless will
Through swine-like frames dispersed to swine-like issues
        still.   ,

But make us men again, for that thou may'st !
Yea, make us men, Enchantress, and restore
These grovelling shapes, degraded and debased,
To fair embodiments of men once more ;—
Yea, by all men that ever woman bore ;—
Yea, e'en by him hereafter born in pain,
Shall draw sustainment from thy bosom's core,
O'er whom thy face yet kindly shall remain,
And find its like therein,—make thou us men again !

The Prayer of the Swine to Circe.

Make thou us men again,—if men but groping
That dark Hereafter which th' Olympians keep ;
Make thou us men again,—if men but hoping
Behind death's doors security of sleep ;—
For yet to laugh is somewhat, and to weep ;—
To feel delight of living, and to plough
The salt-blown acres of the shoreless deep ;—
Better,—yea better far all these than bow
Foul faces to foul earth, and yearn—as we do now !

So they in speech unsyllabled.   But She,
The fair-tressed Goddess, born to be their bane,
Uplifting straight her wand of ivory,
Compelled them groaning to the styes again ;
Where they in hopeless bitterness were fain
To rend the oaken woodwork as before,
And tear the troughs in impotence of pain,—
Not knowing, they, that even at the door
Divine Odysseus stood,—as Hermes told of yore.

THE SICK MAN AND THE BIRDS.

ÆGROTUS.

SPRING,—art thou come, O Spring!
  I am too sick for words;
How hast thou heart to sing,
  O Spring, with all thy birds?

MERULA.

I sing for joy to see again
The merry leaves along the lane,
  The little bud grown ripe;
And look, my love upon the bough!
Hark, how she calleth to me now,—
                "Pipe! pipe!"

ÆGROTUS.

Ah! weary is the sun:
  Love is an idle thing;
But, Bird, thou restless one,
  What ails thee, wandering?

211

The Sick Man and the Birds.

HIRUNDO.

By shore and sea I come and go
To seek I know not what; and lo!
   On no man's eaves I sit
But voices bid me rise once more,
To flit again by sea and shore,—
           Flit! Flit!

ÆGROTUS.

This is Earth's bitter cup:—
   Only to seek, not know.
But Thou, that strivest up,
   Why dost thou carol so?

ALAUDA.

A secret Spirit gifteth me
With song, and wind that lifteth me,—
   A Spirit for whose sake,
Striving amain to reach the sky,
Still to the old dark earth I cry,—
          "Wake! wake!"

ÆGROTUS.

My hope hath lost its wing.
   Thou, that to Night dost call,
How hast thou heart to sing
   Thy tears made musical?

The Sick Man and the Birds.

PHILOMELA.

Alas for me! a dry desire
Is all my song,—a waste of fire
   That will not fade nor fail;
To me, dim shapes of ancient crime
Moan through the windy ways of time,
           "Wail! wail!"

ÆGROTUS.

This is the sick man's song,—
   Mournful, in sooth, and fit;
Unrest that cries " How long!"—
   And the Night answers it.

213

A FLOWER SONG OF ANGIOLA.

Down where the garden grows,
    Gay as a banner,
Spake to her mate the Rose
    After this manner :—
" We are the first of flowers,
    Plain-land or hilly,
All reds and whites are ours,
    Are they not, Lily ? "

Then to the flowers I spake,—
    " Watch ye my Lady
Gone to the leafy brake,
    Silent and shady ;
When I am near to her,
    Lily, she knows ;
How I am dear to her,
    Look to it, Rose."

A Flower Song of Angiola.

Straightway the Blue-bell stooped,
    Paler for pride,
Down where the Violet drooped,
    Shy, at her side:—
" Sweetheart, save me and you,
    Where has the summer kist
Flowers of as fair a hue,—
    Turkis or Amethyst?"

Therewith I laughed aloud,
    Spake on this wise,
" O little flowers so proud,
    Have ye seen eyes
Change through the blue in them,—
    Change till the mere
Loving that grew in them
    Turned to a tear?

" Flowers, ye are bright of hue,
    Delicate, sweet;
Flowers, and the sight of you
    Lightens men's feet;
Yea; but her worth to me,
    Flowerets, even,
Sweetening the earth to me,
    Sweeteneth heaven.

A Flower Song of Angiola.

" This, then, O Flowers, I sing;
    God, when He made ye
Made yet a fairer thing
    Making my Lady;—
Fashioned her tenderly,
    Giving all weal to her;—
Girdle ye slenderly,
    Go to her, kneel to her,—

" Saying, ' He sendeth us,
    He the most dutiful,
Meetly he endeth us,
    Maiden most beautiful!
Let us get rest of you,
    Sweet, in your breast;—
Die, being prest of you,
    Die, being blest.'"

A SONG OF ANGIOLA IN HEAVEN.

FLOWERS,—that have died upon my Sweet
Lulled by the rhythmic dancing beat
  Of her young bosom under you,—
Now will I show you such a thing
As never, through thick buds of Spring,
  Betwixt the daylight and the dew,
The Bird whose being no man knows—
   The voice that waketh all night through,
      Tells to the Rose.

For lo,—a garden-place I found,
Well filled of leaves, and stilled of sound,
  Well flowered, with red fruit marvellous;
And 'twixt the shining trunks would flit
Tall knights and silken maids, or sit
  With faces bent and amorous;—
There, in the heart thereof, and crowned
  With woodbine and amaracus,
      My Love I found.

A Song of Angiola in Heaven.

Alone she walked,—ah, well I wis,
My heart leapt up for joy of this !—
   Then when I called to her her name,—
The name, that like a pleasant thing
Men's lips remember, murmuring,
   At once across the sward she came,—
Full fain she seemed, my own dear maid,
   And askèd ever as she came,
       "Where hast thou stayed?"

"Where hast thou stayed?"—she asked as though
The long years were an hour ago;
   But I spake not, nor answerèd,
For, looking in her eyes, I saw,
A light not lit of mortal law;
   And in her clear cheek's changeless red,
And sweet, unshaken speaking found
   That in this place the Hours were dead,
       And Time was bound.

"This is well done,"—she said,—"in thee,
O Love, that thou art come to me,
   To this green garden glorious;
Now truly shall our life be sped
In joyance and all goodlihed,
   For here all things are fair to us,

A Song of Angiola in Heaven.

And none with burden is oppressed,
  And none is poor or piteous,—
    For here is Rest.

" No formless Future blurs the sky;
  Men mourn not here, with dull dead eye,
    By shrouded shapes of Yesterday;
  Betwixt the Coming and the Past
  The flawless life hangs fixen fast
    In one unwearying To-Day,
  That darkens not; for Sin is shriven,
    Death from the doors is thrust away,
      And here is Heaven."

At "Heaven" she ceased;—and lifted up
Her fair head like a flower-cup,
  With rounded mouth, and eyes aglow;
Then set I lips to hers, and felt,—
Ah, God,—the hard pain fade and melt,
  And past things change to painted show;
The song of quiring birds outbroke;
  The lit leaves laughed,—sky shook, and lo,
    I swooned,—and woke.

And now, O Flowers,
  —Ye that indeed are dead,—

A Song of Angiola in Heaven.

Now for all waiting hours,
　　Well am I comforted;
For of a surety, now, I see,
　　That, without dim distress
　　Of tears, or weariness,
My Lady, verily, awaiteth me;
So that until with Her I be,
　　For my dear Lady's sake
　　I am right fain to make
Out from my pain a pillow, and to take
　Grief for a golden garment unto me;
　　Knowing that I, at last, shall stand
　　In that green garden-land,
And, in the holding of my dear Love's hand,
　Forget the grieving and the misery.

220

THE DYING OF TANNEGUY DU BOIS.

" En los nidas antano no hay pajaros hogano."
—Last Words of Don Quixote.

Yea, I am passed away, I think, from this;
   Nor helps me herb, nor any leechcraft here,
But lift me hither the sweet cross to kiss,
   And witness ye, I go without a fear.
Yea, I am sped, and never more shall see,
   As once I dreamed, the show of shield and crest,
Gone southward to the fighting by the sea;—
   There is no bird in any last year's nest!

Yea, with me now all dreams are done, I ween,
   Grown faint and unremembered; voices call
High up, like misty warders dimly seen
   Moving at morn on some Burgundian wall;
And all things swim—as when the charger stands
   Quivering between the knees, and East and West
Are filled with flash of scarves and waving hands;—
   There is no bird in any last year's nest!

221

The Dying of Tanneguy du Bois.

Is she a dream I left in Aquitaine?—
    My wife Giselle,—who never spoke a word,
Although I knew her mouth was drawn with pain,
    Her eyelids hung with tears; and though I heard
The strong sob shake her throat, and saw the cord
    Her necklace made about it;—she that prest
To watch me trotting till I reached the ford;—
    There is no bird in any last year's nest!

Ah! I had hoped, God wot,—had longed that she
    Should watch me from the little-lit tourelle,
Me, coming riding by the windy lea—
    Me, coming back again to her, Giselle;
Yea, I had hoped once more to hear him call,
    The curly-pate, who, rushen lance in rest,
Stormed at the lilies by the orchard wall;—
    There is no bird in any last year's nest!

But how, my Masters, ye are wrapt in gloom!
    This Death will come, and whom he loves he cleaves
Sheer through the steel and leather; hating whom
    He smites in shameful wise behind the greaves.
'T is a fair time with Dennis and the Saints,
    And weary work to age, and want for rest,
When harness groweth heavy, and one faints,
    With no bird left in any last year's nest!

The Dying of Tanneguy du Bois.

Give ye good hap, then, all.   For me, I lie
  Broken in Christ's sweet hand, with whom shall rest
To keep me living, now that I must die;—
  There is no bird in any last year's nest!

THE MOSQUE OF THE CALIPH.

Unto Seyd the vizier spake the Caliph Abdallah :—
" Now hearken and hear, I am weary, by Allah!
I am faint with the mere over-running of leisure;
I will rouse me and rear up a palace to Pleasure!"

To Abdallah the Caliph spake Seyd the vizier:—
" All faces grow pale if my Lord draweth near;
And the breath of his mouth not a mortal shall scoff
     it;—
They must bend and obey, by the beard of the
     Prophet!"

Then the Caliph that heard, with becoming sedate-
     ness,
Drew his hand down *his* beard as he thought of his
     greatness;
Drained out the last bead of the wine in the chalice:
" I have spoken, O Seyd; I will build it, my palace!

" As a drop from the wine where the wine-cup hath
  spilled it,
As a gem from the mine,—O my Seyd, I will build
  it ; ·
Without price, without flaw, it shall stand for a token
That the word is a law which the Caliph hath
  spoken ! "

Yet again to the Caliph bent Seyd the vizier :
" Who shall reason or rail if my Lord speaketh clear ?
Who shall strive with his might ? Let my Lord live
  for ever !
He shall choose him a site by the side of the river."

Then the Caliph sent forth unto Kür, unto Yemen,—
To the South, to the North,—for the skilfullest free-
  men ;
And soon, in a close, where the river breeze fanned it,
The basement uprose, as the Caliph had planned it.

Now the courses were laid and the corner-piece
  fitted ;
And the butments and set-stones were shapen and
  knitted,
When lo ! on a sudden the Caliph heard frowning,
That the river had swelled, and the workmen were
  drowning.

Then the Caliph was stirred and he flushed in his ire
as
He sent forth his word from Teheran to Shiraz;
And the workmen came new, and the palace, built
faster,
From the bases up-grew unto arch and pilaster.

And the groinings were traced, and the arch-heads
were chasen,
When lo! in hot haste there came flying a mason,
For a cupola fallen had whelmed half the workmen;
And Hamet the chief had been slain by the Turc'-
men.

Then the Caliph's beard curled, and he foamed in his
rage as
Once more his scouts whirled from the Tell to the
Hedjaz;
"Is my word not my word?" cried the Caliph Ab-
dallah;
"I *will* build it up yet ... *by the aiding of Allah!*"

Though he spoke in his haste like King David before
him,
Yet he felt as he spoke that a something stole o'er
him;

And his soul grew as glass, and his anger passed from
     it
As the vapours that pass from the Pool of Mahomet.

And the doom seemed to hang on the palace no
     longer,
Like a fountain it sprang when the sources feed
     stronger;
Shaft, turret and spire leaped upward, diminished
Like the flames of a fire,—till the palace was fin-
     ished!

Without price, without flaw. And it lay on the azure
Like a diadem dropped from an emperor's treasure;
And the dome of pearl white and the pinnacles
     fleckless,
Flashed back to the light, like the gems in a neck-
     lace.

So the Caliph looked forth on the turret-tops gilded;
And he said in his pride, " Is my palace not builded?
Who is more great than I that his word can avail if
My will is my will,"—said Abdallah the Caliph.

But lo! with the light he repented his scorning,
For an earthquake had shattered the whole ere the
     morning;

The Mosque of the Caliph.

Of the pearl-coloured dome there was left but a
    ruin,—
But an arch as a home for the ring-dove to coo in.

Shaft, turret and spire—all were tumbled and crum-
    bled;
And the soul of the Caliph within him was humbled;
And he bowed in the dust:—"There is none great
    but Allah!
I will build Him a Mosque,"—said the Caliph Ab-
    dallah.

And the Caliph has gone to his fathers for ever,
But the Mosque that he builded shines still by the
    river;
And the pilgrims up-stream to this day slacken sail if
They catch the first gleam of the "Mosque of the
    Caliph."

IN THE BELFRY.

WRITTEN UNDER RETHEL'S "DEATH, THE FRIEND."

TOLL!   Is it night, or daylight yet?
Somewhere the birds seem singing still,
Though surely now the sun has set.

Toll!   But who tolls the Bell once more?
He must have climbed the parapet.
Did I not bar the belfry door?

Who can it be?—the Bernardine,
That used to pray with me of yore?
No,—for the monk was not so lean.

This must be He who, legend saith,
Comes sometimes with a kindlier mien
And tolls a knell.—This shape is Death.

Good-bye, old Bell!   So let it be.
How strangely now I draw my breath!
What is this haze of light I see? . . .

IN MANUS TUAS, DOMINE!

ESSAYS IN OLD-FRENCH FORMS

"They are a school to win
The fair French daughter to learn English in;
And, gracèd with her song,
To make the language sweet upon her tongue."

BEN JONSON, Underwoods.

[*With a view to indicate the capabilities of these old-French forms of verse in abler hands, the examples here given have been made as various as possible. They have been so recently discussed in English and American periodicals, and are besides so fully described in the treatises of M.* THEODORE DE BANVILLE *and Count* FERDINAND DE GRAMONT *that it is not necessary to enter into any detailed account of them in this place. As, however, the form of Villanelle here written differs slightly from that first followed by the Author, it is proper to add that he has been convinced by the arguments of M.* JOSEPH BOULMIER, *the most accomplished of modern French "villanelliers," that it is not wise to depart in this case from the well-known model of* PASSERAT. *("Ja'i perdu ma tourtourelle.")*]

ROSE-LEAVES.

(TRIOLETS.)

"Sans peser.—Sans rester."

These are leaves of my rose,
Pink petals I treasure :
There is more than one knows
In these leaves of my rose ;
O the joys !   O the woes !
They are quite beyond measure.
These are leaves of my rose,—
Pink petals I treasure.

A KISS.

ROSE kissed me to-day.
    Will she kiss me to-morrow?
Let it be as it may,
Rose kissed me to-day.

233

But the pleasure gives way
　　To a savour of sorrow ;—
Rose kissed me to-day,—
　　Will she kiss me to-morrow ?

CIRCE.

IN the School of Coquettes
　　Madam Rose is a scholar :—
O, they fish with all nets
In the School of Coquettes !
When her brooch she forgets
　　'T is to show her new collar ;
In the School of Coquettes
　　Madam Rose is a scholar !

A TEAR.

THERE 's a tear in her eye,—
　　Such a clear little jewel !
What on earth makes her cry ?
There 's a tear in her eye.
" Puck has killed a big fly,—
　　And it 's *horribly* cruel ; "
There 's a tear in her eye,—
　　Such a clear little jewel !

"AMARI ALIQUID."

"WILL you hear 'All Alone'?"—
  "No, I think I quite know it."
"But you liked it, my Own?"—
  "When I *was*—'all alone'!
Now that season has flown;
  And besides—*I've the Poet!*"—
"Will you hear 'All Alone'?"
"No, I think I *quite* know it."

A GREEK GIFT.

HERE's a present for Rose,
  How pleased she is looking!
Is it verse?—is it prose?
Here's a present for Rose!
"*Plats*," "*Entrées*," and "*Rôts*,"—
  Why, it's "Gouffé on Cooking"!
Here's a present for Rose,
  How *pleased* she is looking!

OLD LOVES.

"THEN, you liked little Bowes"—
  "And you liked Jane Raby!"
"But you like *me* now, Rose?"
"As I liked 'little Bowes'!"

235

" Am I then to suppose ? "—

   " *Hush !—you must n't wake Baby !* "

" *Did* you like little Bowes ? "—

   " If you liked Jane Raby ! "

      " URCEUS EXIT."

I INTENDED an Ode,

   And it turned to a Sonnet.

It began *à la mode*,

I intended an Ode ;

But Rose crossed the road

   In her latest new bonnet ;

I intended an Ode,

   And it turned to a Sonnet.

"PERSICOS ODI."

(TRIOLETS.)

Davus, I detest
  Orient display;
Wreaths on linden drest,
Davus, I detest.
Let the late rose rest
  Where it fades away:—
Davus, I detest
  Orient display.

Naught but myrtle twine
  Therefore, Boy, for me
Sitting 'neath the vine,—
Naught but myrtle twine;
Fitting to the wine,
  Not unfitting thee;
Naught but myrtle twine
  Therefore, Boy, for me.

THE WANDERER.

(RONDEL.)

Love comes back to his vacant dwelling,—
   The old, old Love that we knew of yore!
   We see him stand by the open door,
With his great eyes sad, and his bosom swelling.

He makes as though in our arms repelling,
   He fain would lie as he lay before;—
Love comes back to his vacant dwelling,—
   The old, old Love that we knew of yore!

Ah, who shall help us from over-telling
   That sweet forgotten, forbidden lore!
   E'en as we doubt in our heart once more,
With a rush of tears to our eyelids welling,
Love comes back to his vacant dwelling.

"VITAS HINNULEO."

(RONDEL.)

You shun me, Chloe, wild and shy
　　As some stray fawn that seeks its mother
Through trackless woods.　If spring-winds sigh
　　It vainly strives its fears to smother;—

Its trembling knees assail each other
　　When lizards stir the bramble dry;—
　　You shun me, Chloe, wild and shy
As some stray fawn that seeks its mother.

And yet no Libyan lion I,—
　　No ravening thing to rend another;
Lay by your tears, your tremors by—
　　A Husband 's better than a brother;
Nor shun me, Chloe, wild and shy
　　As some stray fawn that seeks its mother.

"ON LONDON STONES."

(RONDEAU.)

ON London stones I sometimes sigh
For wider green and bluer sky;—
 Too oft the trembling note is drowned
 In this huge city's varied sound;—
" Pure song is country-born "—I cry.

Then comes the spring,—the months go by,
The last stray swallows seaward fly;
 And I—I too!—no more am found
 On London stones!

In vain!—the woods, the fields deny
That clearer strain I fain would try;
 Mine is an urban Muse, and bound
 By some strange law to paven ground;
Abroad she pouts;—she is not shy
 On London stones!

"FAREWELL, RENOWN!"

(RONDEAU.)

FAREWELL, Renown! Too fleeting flower,
That grows a year to last an hour;—
   Prize of the race's dust and heat,
   Too often trodden under feet,—
Why should I court your "barren dower"?

Nay;—had I Dryden's angry power,—
The thews of Ben,—the wind of Gower,—
   Not less my voice should still repeat
      "Farewell, Renown!"

Farewell!—Because the Muses' bower
Is filled with rival brows that lower;—
   Because, howe'er his pipe be sweet,
   The Bard, that "pays," must please the street;—
But most . . . because the grapes are sour,—
      Farewell, Renown!

"MORE POETS YET!"

(RONDEAU.)

" MORE Poets yet!"—I hear him say,
  Arming his heavy hand to slay;—
    " Despite my skill and 'swashing blow,'
     They seem to sprout where'er I go;—
I killed a host but yesterday!"

Slash on, O Hercules! You may.
Your task 's, at best, a Hydra-fray;
    And though *you* cut, not less will grow
        More Poets yet!

Too arrogant! For who shall stay
The first blind motions of the May?
    Who shall out-blot the morning glow?—
    Or stem the full heart's overflow?
Who? There will rise, till Time decay,
        More Poets yet!

"WITH PIPE AND FLUTE."

(RONDEAU.)

WITH pipe and flute the rustic Pan
Of old made music sweet for man;
   And wonder hushed the warbling bird,
   And closer drew the calm-eyed herd,—
The rolling river slowlier ran.

Ah! would,—ah! would, a little span,
Some air of Arcady could fan
   This age of ours, too seldom stirred
          With pipe and flute!

But now for gold we plot and plan;
And from Beersheba unto Dan,
   Apollo's self might pass unheard,
   Or find the night-jar's note preferred;—
Not so it fared, when time began,
          With pipe and flute!

A RONDEAU TO ETHEL,

(Who wishes she had lived—
" In teacup-times of hood and hoop,
Or while the patch was worn.")

"IN teacup times!"   The style of dress
Would suit your beauty, I confess;
   BELINDA-like, the patch you 'd wear;
   I picture you with powdered hair,—
You 'd make a charming Shepherdess!

And I—no doubt—could well express
SIR PLUME's complete conceitedness,—
   Could poise a clouded cane with care
           " In teacup-times!"

The parts would fit precisely—yes:
We should achieve a huge success!
   You should disdain, and I despair,
   With quite the true Augustan air;
But . . . could I love you more, or less,—
           " In teacup-times?"

"O FONS BANDUSIÆ."

(RONDEAU.)

O BABBLING Spring, than glass more clear,
Worthy of wreath and cup sincere,
   To-morrow shall a kid be thine
   With swelled and sprouting brows for sign,—
Sure sign!—of loves and battles near.

Child of the race that butt and rear!
Not less, alas! his life-blood dear
   Shall tinge thy cold wave crystalline,
         O babbling Spring!

Thee Sirius knows not. Thou dost cheer
With pleasant cool the plough-worn steer,—
   The wandering flock. This verse of mine
   Shall rank thee one with founts divine;
Men shall thy rock and tree revere,
         O babbling Spring!

"VIXI PUELLIS."

(RONDEAU OF VILLON.)

WE loved of yore, in warfare bold,
  Nor laurelless. Now all must go;
  Let this left wall of Venus show
The arms, the tuneless lyre of old.

Here let them hang, the torches cold,
  The portal-bursting bar, the bow,
      We loved of yore.

But thou, who Cyprus sweet dost hold,
  And Memphis free from Thracian snow,
  Goddess and queen, with vengeful blow,
Smite,—smite but once that pretty scold
      We loved of yore.

"WHEN I SAW YOU LAST, ROSE."

(VILLANELLE.)

WHEN I saw you last, Rose,
You were only so high;—
How fast the time goes!

Like a′bud ere it blows,
You just peeped at the sky,
When I saw you last, Rose!

Now your petals unclose,
Now your May-time is nigh;—
How fast the time goes!

And a life,—how it grows!
You were scarcely so shy,
When I saw you last, Rose!

247

"When I Saw you Last, Rose."

In your bosom it shows
There 's a guest on the sly;
(How fast the time goes!)

Is it Cupid?   Who knows!
Yet you used not to sigh,
When I saw you last, Rose!
How fast the time goes!

FOR A COPY OF THEOCRITUS.

(VILLANELLE.)

O SINGER of the field and fold,
THEOCRITUS!   Pan's pipe was thine,—
Thine was the happier Age of Gold.

For thee the scent of new-turned mould,
The bee-hives, and the murmuring pine,
O Singer of the field and fold!

Thou sang'st the simple feasts of old,—
The beechen bowl made glad with wine . .
Thine was the happier Age of Gold.

Thou bad'st the rustic loves be told,—
Thou bad'st the tuneful reeds combine,
O Singer of the field and fold!

For a Copy of Theocritus.

And round thee, ever-laughing, rolled
The blithe and blue Sicilian brine . .
Thine was the happier Age of Gold.

Alas for us!   Our songs are cold;
Our Northern suns too sadly shine :—
O Singer of the field and fold,
Thine was the happier Age of Gold!

"TU NE QUAESIERIS."

(VILLANELLE.)

SEEK not, O Maid, to know,
(Alas! unblest the trying!)
When thou and I must go.

No lore of stars can show.
What shall be, vainly prying,
Seek not, O Maid, to know.

Will Jove long years bestow?—
Or is 't with this one dying,
That thou and I must go;

Now,—when the great winds blow,
And waves the reef are plying? . .
Seek not, O Maid, to know.

"*Tu ne Quaesieris.*"

Rather let clear wine flow,
On no vain hope relying;
When thou and I must go

Lies dark;—then be it so.
Now,—*now*, churl Time is flying;
Seek not, O Maid, to know
When thou and I must go.

252

A SONNET IN DIALOGUE.

FRANK *(on the Lawn).*
Come to the Terrace, May,—the sun is low.

MAY *(in the House).*
Thanks, I prefer my Browning here instead.

FRANK.
There are two peaches by the strawberry bed.

MAY.
They will be riper if we let them grow.

FRANK.
Then the Park-aloe is in bloom, you know.

MAY.
Also, her Majesty Queen Anne is dead.

FRANK.
But surely, May, your pony must be fed.

A Sonnet in Dialogue.

MAY.

And was, and is.   I fed him hours ago.
'T is useless, Frank, you see I shall not stir.

FRANK.

Still, I had something you would like to hear.

MAY.

No doubt some new frivolity of men.

FRANK.

Nay,—'t is a thing the gentler sex deplores
Chiefly, I think . . .

MAY *(coming to the window)*.
What is this secret, then ?

FRANK *(mysteriously)*.
There are no eyes more beautiful than yours!

254

LOVE'S FAREWELL.

(HUITAIN.)

"No more!"—I said to Love. "No more!
I scorn your baby-arts to know!
Not now am I as once of yore;
My brow the Sage's line can show!"
"Farewell!"—he laughed. "Farewell! I go!"
And clove the air with fluttering track:
"Farewell!"—he cried far off; but lo!
He sent a Parthian arrow back!

255

A CASE OF CAMEOS.

(DIXAINS.)

AGATE.

(*The Power of Love.*)

FIRST, in an Agate-stone, a Centaur strong,
With square man-breasts and hide of dapple dun,
His brown arms bound behind him with a thong,
On strained croup strove to free himself from one,—
A bolder rider than Bellerophon.
For, on his back, by some strange power of art,
There sat a laughing Boy with bow and dart,
Who drove him where he would, and driving him,
With that barbed toy would make him rear and start.
To this was writ "World-victor" on the rim.

CHALCEDONY.

(The Thefts of Mercury.)

THE next in legend bade " Beware of show ! "
'T was graven this on pale Chalcedony.
Here great Apollo, with unbended bow,
His quiver hard by on a laurel tree,
For some new theft was rating Mercury.
Who stood with downcast eyes, and feigned distress,
As daring not, for utter guiltiness,
To meet that angry voice and aspect joined.
His very heel-wings drooped; but yet, not less,
His backward hand the Sun-God's shafts purloined.

SARDONYX.

(The Song of Orpheus.)

THEN, on a Sardonyx, the man of Thrace,
The voice supreme that through Hell's portals stole,
With carved white lyre and glorious song-lit face,
(Too soon, alas ! on Hebrus' wave to roll !)
Played to the beasts, from a great elm-tree bole.
And lo ! with half-shut eyes the leopard spread
His lissome length; and deer with gentle tread
Came through the trees; and, from a nearer spring,
The prick-eared rabbit paused; while overhead
The stock-dove drifted downward, fluttering.

A Case of Cameos.

AMETHYST.

(The Crowning of Silenus.)

NEXT came an Amethyst,—the grape in hue.
On a mock throne, by fresh excess disgraced,
With heavy head, and thyrsus held askew,
The Youths, in scorn, had dull Silenus placed,
And o'er him "King of Topers" they had traced.
Yet but a King of Sleep he seemed at best,
With wine-bag cheeks that bulged upon his breast,
And vat-like paunch distent from his carouse.
Meanwhile, his ass, by no respect represt,
Munched at the wreath upon her Master's brows.

BERYL.

(The Sirens.)

LASTLY, with "Pleasure" was a Beryl graven,
Clear-hued,—divine.   Thereon the Sirens sung.
What time, beneath, by rough rock-bases caven,
And jaw-like rifts where many a green bone clung,
The strong flood-tide, in-rushing, coiled and swung.
Then,—in the offing,—on the lift o' the sea,
A tall ship drawing shoreward, helplessly.
For, from the prow, e'en now the rowers leap
Headlong, nor seek from that sweet fate to flee . . .
Ah me, those Women-witches of the Deep!

THE PRODIGALS.

(BALLADE: IRREGULAR.)

" PRINCES !—and you, most valorous,
    Nobles !—and Barons of all degrees !
Hearken awhile to the prayer of us,—
    Beggars that come from the over-seas !
    Nothing we ask or of gold or fees;
Harry us not with the hounds we pray ;
    Lo,—for the surcote's hem we seize,—
Give us—ah! give us—but Yesterday ! "

" Dames most delicate, amorous !
    Damosels blithe as the belted bees !
Hearken awhile to the prayer of us,—
    Beggars that come from the over-seas !
    Nothing we ask of the things that please;
Weary are we, and worn, and gray ;
    Lo,—for we clutch and we clasp your knees,—
Give us—ah! give us—but Yesterday ! "

The Prodigals.

" Damosels—Dames, be piteous ! "
    (But the dames rode fast by the roadway trees.
" Hear us, O Knights magnanimous ! "
    (But the knights pricked on in their panoplies.)
    Nothing they gat or of hope or ease,
  But only to beat on the breast and say :—
  " Life we drank to the dregs and lees ;
  Give us—ah ! give us—but Yesterday ! "

ENVOY.

  YOUTH, take heed to the prayer of these !
  Many there be by the dusty way,—
    Many that cry to the rocks and seas
  " Give us—ah ! give us—but Yesterday ! "

THE BALLAD OF THE BARMECIDE.

(BALLADE.)

To one in Eastern clime,—'t is said,—
   There came a man at eve with "Lo!
Friend, ere the day be dimmed and dead,
   Hast thou a mind to feast, and know
   Fair cates, and sweet wine's overflow?"
To whom that other fain replied—
   "Lead on.   Not backward I nor slow;—
Where is thy feast, O Barmecide?"

Thereon the bidder passed and led
   To where, apart from dust and glow,
They found a board with napery spread,
   And gold, and glistering cups a-row.
   "Eat," quoth the host, yet naught did show.
To whom his guest—"Thy board is wide;
   But barren is the cheer, I trow;
Where is thy feast, O Barmecide?"

The Ballad of the Barmecide.

"Eat"—quoth the man not less, and fed
    From meats unseen, and made as though
He drank of wine both white and red.
    "Eat,—ere the day to darkness grow.
      Short space and scant the Fates bestow!"
What time his guest him wondering eyed,
    Muttering in wrath his beard below—
"Where is thy feast, O Barmecide?"

ENVOY.

Time,—'t is of thee they fable so.
    Thou bidd'st us eat, and still denied,
Still fasting, from thy board we go:—
    "Where is *thy* feast, O Barmecide?"

ON A FAN THAT BELONGED TO THE MARQUISE DE POMPADOUR.

(BALLADE.)

CHICKEN-SKIN, delicate, white,
  Painted by Carlo Vanloo,
Loves in a riot of light,
  Roses and vaporous blue;
  Hark to the dainty *frou-frou!*
Picture above, if you can,
  Eyes that could melt as the dew,—
This was the Pompadour's fan !

See how they rise at the sight,
  Thronging the *Œil de Bœuf* through,
Courtiers as butterflies bright,
  Beauties that Fragonard drew,
  Talon-rouge, falbala, queue,
Cardinal, Duke,—to a man,
  Eager to sigh or to sue,—
This was the Pompadour's fan !

The Fan of the Marquise de Pompadour.

Ah, but things more than polite
    Hung on this toy, *voyez-vous !*
Matters of state and of might,
    Things that great ministers do;
    Things that, may be, overthrew
Those in whose brains they began;
    Here was the sign and the cue,—
This was the Pompadour's fan !

ENVOY.

WHERE are the secrets it knew ?
    Weavings of plot and of plan ?
—But where is the Pompadour, too ?
    This was the Pompadour's *Fan !*

A BALLAD TO QUEEN ELIZABETH
of the Spanish Armada.

(BALLADE.)

KING PHILLIP had vaunted his claims;
    He had sworn for a year he would sack us;
With an army of heathenish names
    He was coming to fagot and stack us;
    Like the thieves of the sea he would track us,
And shatter our ships on the main;
    But we had bold Neptune to back us,—
And where are the galleons of Spain?

His caracks were christened of dames
    To the kirtles whereof he would tack us;
With his saints and his gilded stern-frames,
    He had thought like an egg-shell to crack us;
    Now Howard may get to his Flaccus,
And Drake to his Devon again,
    And Hawkins bowl rubbers to Bacchus,—
For where are the galleons of Spain?

A Ballad to Queen Elizabeth.

Let his Majesty hang to St. James
    The·axe that he whetted to hack us ;
He must play at some lustier games
    Or at sea he can hope to out-thwack us ;
    To his mines of Peru he would pack us
To tug at his bullet and chain ;
    Alas ! that his Greatness should lack us !—
But where are the galleons of Spain ?

ENVOY.

GLORIANA !—the Don may attack us
Whenever his stomach be fain ;
    He must reach us before he can rack us, . . .
And where are the galleons of Spain ?

THE BALLAD OF IMITATION.

(BALLADE.)

" C'est imiter quelqu'un que de planter des choux."
—ALFRED DE MUSSET.

IF they hint, O Musician, the piece that you played
    Is nought but a copy of Chopin or Spohr;
That the ballad you sing is but merely "conveyed"
    From the stock of the Arnes and the Purcells of yore;
    That there 's nothing, in short, in the words or the
        score
That is not as out-worn as the "Wandering Jew";
    Make answer—Beethoven could scarcely do more—
That the man who plants cabbages imitates, too!

If they tell you, Sir Artist, your light and your shade
    Are simply "adapted" from other men's lore;
That—plainly to speak of a "spade" as a "spade"—
    You 've "stolen" your grouping from three or from
        four;

The Ballad of Imitation.

That, however the writer the truth may deplore,
'T was Gainsborough painted *your* "Little Boy Blue";
    Smile only serenely—though cut to the core—
For the man who plants cabbages imitates, too!

And you too, my Poet, be never dismayed
    If they whisper your Epic—"Sir Éperon d'Or"—
Is nothing but Tennyson thinly arrayed
    In a tissue that 's taken from Morris's store;
    That no one, in fact, but a child could ignore
That you "lift" or "accommodate" all that you do;
    Take heart—though your Pegasus' withers be sore—
For the man who plants cabbages imitates, too!

———

POSTSCRIPTUM.—And you, whom we all so adore,
    Dear Critics, whose verdicts are always so new!—
One word in your ear. There were Critics before . . .
    And the man who plants cabbages imitates, too!

THE BALLAD OF PROSE AND RHYME.

(BALLADE À DOUBLE REFRAIN).

When the ways are heavy with mire and rut,
　In November fogs, in December snows,
When the North Wind howls, and the doors are shut,—
　　There is place and enough for the pains of prose;
　　But whenever a scent from the whitethorn blows,
And the jasmine-stars at the casement climb,
　　And a Rosalind-face at the lattice shows,
Then hey!—for the ripple of laughing rhyme!

When the brain gets dry as an empty nut,
　When the reason stands on its squarest toes,
When the mind (like a beard) has a "formal cut,"—
　　There is place and enough for the pains of prose;
　　But whenever the May-blood stirs and glows,
And the young year draws to the "golden prime,"
　　And Sir Romeo sticks in his ear a rose,—
Then hey!—for the ripple of laughing rhyme!

The Ballad of Prose and Rhyme.

In a theme where the thoughts have a pedant-strut,
  In a changing quarrel of " Ayes " and " Noes,"
In a starched procession of " If " and " But,"—
  There is place and enough for the pains of prose;
  But whenever a soft glance softer grows
And the light hours dance to the trysting-time,
  And the secret is told " that no one knows,"—
Then hey !—for the ripple of laughing rhyme!

ENVOY.

In the work-a-day world,—for its needs and woes,
  There is place and enough for the pains of prose;
But whenever the May-bells clash and chime,
  Then hey !—for the ripple of laughing rhyme!

THE DANCE OF DEATH.

(CHANT ROYAL, AFTER HOLBEIN.)

" Contra vim Mortis
Non est medicamen in hortis."

He is the despots' Despot.   All must bide,
Later or soon, the message of his might;
Princes and potentates their heads must hide,
Touched by the awful sigil of his right;
Beside the Kaiser he at eve doth wait
And pours a potion in his cup of state;
The stately Queen his bidding must obey;
No keen-eyed Cardinal shall him affray;
And to the Dame that wantoneth he saith—
" Let be, Sweet-heart, to junket and to play."
There is no king more terrible than Death.

The lusty Lord, rejoicing in his pride,
He draweth down; before the armèd Knight

271

The Dance of Death.

With jingling bridle-rein he still doth ride;
He crosseth the strong Captain in the fight;
He beckons the grave Elder from debate;
He hales the Abbot by his shaven pate,
Nor for the Abbess' wailing will delay;
No bawling Mendicant shall say him nay;
E'en to the pyx the Priest he followeth,
Nor can the Leech his chilling finger stay ..
There is no king more terrible than Death.

All things must bow to him.   And woe betide
The Wine-bibber,—the Roysterer by night;
Him the feast-master, many bouts defied,
Him 'twixt the pledging and the cup shall smite;
Woe to the Lender at usurious rate,
The hard Rich Man, the hireling Advocate;
Woe to the Judge that selleth right for pay;
Woe to the Thief that like a beast of prey
With creeping tread the traveller harryeth :—
These, in their sin, the sudden sword shall slay ..
There is no king more terrible than Death.

He hath no pity,—nor will be denied.
When the low hearth is garnishèd and bright,
Grimly he flingeth the dim portal wide,
And steals the Infant in the Mother's sight;

The Dance of Death.

He hath no pity for the scorned of fate:—
He spares not Lazarus lying at the gate, ·
Nay, nor the Blind that stumbleth as he may;
Nay, the tired Ploughman,—at the sinking ray,—
In the last furrow,—feels an icy breath,
And knows a hand hath turned the team astray ..
There is no king more terrible than Death.

He hath no pity.   For the new-made Bride,
Blithe with the promise of her life and light,
That wanders gladly by her Husband's side,
He with the clatter of his drum doth fright;
He scares the Virgin at the convent grate;
The Maid half-won, the Lover passionate;
He hath no grace for weakness and decay:
The tender Wife, the Widow bent and gray,
The feeble Sire whose footstep faltereth,—
All these he leadeth by the lonely way ..
There is no king more terrible than Death.

ENVOY.

YOUTH, for whose ear and monishing of late,
I sang of Prodigals and lost estate,
Have thou thy joy of living and be gay;

But know not less that there must come a day,—
Aye, and perchance e'en now it hasteneth,—
When thine own heart shall speak to thee and
   . say,—
There is no king more terrible than Death.

ARS VICTRIX.

(IMITATED FROM THÉOPHILE GAUTIER.)

Yes; when the ways oppose—
　　When the hard means rebel,
Fairer the work out-grows,—
　　More potent far the spell.

O Poet, then, forbear
　　The loosely-sandalled verse,
Choose rather thou to wear
　　The buskin—straight and terse;

Leave to the tiro's hand
　　The limp and shapeless style;
See that thy form demand
　　The labour of the file.

Ars Victrix.

Sculptor, do thou discard
   The yielding clay,—consign
To Paros marble hard
   The beauty of thy line;—

Model thy Satyr's face
   In bronze of Syracuse;
In the veined agate trace
   The profile of thy Muse.

Painter, that still must mix
   But transient tints anew,
Thou in the furnace fix
   The firm enamel's hue;

Let the smooth tile receive
   Thy dove-drawn Erycine;
Thy Sirens blue at eve
   Coiled in a wash of wine.

All passes. ART alone
   Enduring stays to us;
The Bust out-lasts the throne,—
   The Coin, Tiberius;

Ars Victrix.

Even the gods must go ;
  Only the lofty Rhyme
Not countless years o'erthrow,—
  Not long array of time.

Paint, chisel, then, or write ;
  But, that the work surpass,
With the hard fashion fight,—
  With the resisting mass.

277

When Finis *comes, the Book we close,*
And somewhat sadly, Fancy goes,
  With backward step, from stage to stage
  Of that accomplished pilgrimage . . .
The thorn lies thicker than the rose!

There is so much that no one knows,—
So much un-reached that none suppose;
  What flaws! what faults!—on every page,
        When Finis *comes.*

Still,—they must pass! The swift Tide flows.
Though not for all the laurel grows,
  Perchance, in this be-slandered age,
  The worker, mainly, wins his wage;—
And Time will sweep both friends and foes
        When FINIS *comes!*

DOBSON'S (AUSTIN) VIGNETTES IN RHYME.
With an Introduction by E. C. STEDMAN. Square 12mo, gilt,
$2.00

"Has been classed with Praed and Locker, but he has a greater mastery of rhythm than the one, a wider range than the other, and, at his best, he rises into an atmosphere which neither of these writers has frequently breathed. He is a very fresh, polished, and graceful poet, whose right to a seat in the choir is as incontestable as that of the leading singer."—*Atlantic Monthly.*

"One of the most exquisitely delightful of books. If Mr. Austin Dobson writes nothing but the two volumes he has already given to the world, he will have an enduring place of his own in poetic literature."—*London Contemporary Review.*

"We were hardly prepared for the touches of genuine beauty which adorn so many of these little poems, and set the verses of 'society' in a framework of softer and more imaginative loveliness than the refined give-and-take of social intellect and sentiment usually suggest."—*London Spectator.*

VERS DE SOCIÉTÉ, by Praed, Landor, Thackeray, Moore, Holmes, Calverley, Saxe, Locker, Dobson, and the other recent authors in this department. Selected by CHARLES H. JONES, with illustrated title and vignettes, drawn by JOHN A. MITCHELL, and engraved by HENRY MARSH. 8vo. Cloth, gilt. $4.00. Full Levant morocco, $9.00. The same, without vignettes. 16mo. (Leisure Hour Series.) $1.00.

"A more beautiful and every way delightful gift-book for Christmas or any other season would be difficult to conceive. Wit, sentiment, poetry, and art, are therein combined in the most felicitous proportions. It is such a collection of this class of poems, a class that has only lately been distinctly recognized and cultivated, as was never before made, and it may be said to include nearly everything that ought to have a place in such an anthology."—*Boston Advertiser.*

"If we have ever seen a daintier piece of book-making, we have forgotten it."
—*Evening Post.*

CALVERLEY'S (C. S.) FLY-LEAVES. With additions from the author's earlier volume of Verses and Translations. Third edition, with a new poem. 16mo. (Leisure Hour Series.) $1.00.

"As pleasant a book of light, humorous poetry as we have seen in a long time, and which we heartily commend to the attention of all our readers."—*Nation.*

LIBRARY OF FOREIGN POETRY. 16mo. Cloth, gilt top and side stamp, bevelled edges.

    I. **Herz's King René's Daughter.** $1.25.

    II. **Tegner's Frithiof's Saga.** $1.50.

  III. **Lessing's Nathan the Wise.** $1.50.

  IV. **Selections from the Kalevala.** $1.50.

    V. **Heine's Book of Songs.** $1.50.

  VI. **Goethe's Poems and Ballads.** $1.50.

 VII. **Lockhart's Ancient Spanish Ballads.** $1.25.

JOHNSON'S (ROSSITER) COLLECTION OF POEMS.
Famous Single and Fugitive Poems. Collected and Edited by ROSSITER JOHNSON. New edition, revised and enlarged. Square 12mo, gilt. $2.00.

A pretty volume, fit for presentation, made up of celebrated English poems that have hitherto been printed only in periodicals and other fugitive places, or are in only such works as are not generally at hand.

The lover of poetry who is trying to find some English poem that he can get no trace of except from vague memory, would be quite apt to meet it in this volume.

Play-Day Poems, collected and edited by ROSSITER JOHNSON. 16mo. (Leisure Hour Series.) $1.00.

This volume contains the best of the humorous poetry published since Parton's collection in 1856, and also many of the old favorites.

"Singularly free from anything to offend the taste, or to injure the health by unsuccessful attempts to produce a laugh. You are not obliged to throw away a multitude of worthless or mediocre specimens, before you light upon a poem which you can truly enjoy."—*N. Y. Tribune.*

McKNIGHT'S (GEORGE) LIFE AND FAITH. Life
and Faith. Sonnets. By George McKnight. Square 12mo. $2.00.

"A book to which one can turn with hearty pleasure. A book rich in thought. His thoughts are absolutely his own. He has worked out many of the hardest problems of the age, and always with a sweetness and candor that win our love; while his bold touches often carry us to the very heart of thought, though with a perpetual tendency to the larger and more hopeful view. And sometimes there are really fine imaginative touches."—*Nation.*

"We can commend it sincerely to thoughtful and meditative people as a volume which they can hardly open anywhere without the pleasure that comes from the expression of a gentle, courageous, and lucid mind."—*Atlantic Monthly.*

SWINBURNE'S (A. C.) WORKS.

> **The Queen Mother and Rosamond.** 16mo. $1.50.
>
> **Chastelard.** A Tragedy. 16mo, cloth. $1.25.
>
> **Atalanta in Calydon.** 1 vol. 16mo. $1.25.

"The greatest modern reproduction of Greek tragedy."—*Westminster Review.*

COLLEGE HYMNAL, THE. A Book of Sacred Song,
selected from the best English Authors. 18mo. $1.25.

This new Hymnal contains over five hundred selections, with the author's name and the name of an appropriate tune prefixed to each hymn. It also has the usual indexes.

SMITH'S (H. & J.) REJECTED ADDRESSES; or, The
New Theatrum Poetarum. With Preface and Notes by the Authors. 16mo. (Leisure-Hour Series.) $1.00.

"One of the raciest and wittiest works of the age."—*London Times.*

THE AMATEUR SERIES. 12mo, blue cloth.

Hector Berlioz. Selections from his Letters, and Æsthetic, Humorous, and Satirical Writings. Translated, and preceded by a Biographical Sketch of the Author. By WILLIAM F. APTHORP. $2.00.

" Is read with surprise, and put aside when the last page is finished with reluctance. Full of anecdote and rich with individuality, the biography gives genuine pleasure."—*Art Interchange.*

English Actors from Shakespeare to Macready. By HENRY BARTON BAKER. Two vols. $3.50.

" The book is extremely rich in good stories, which are invariably well told."—*Pall Mall Gazette.*

Moscheles' (Ignatz) Recent Music and Musicians, as described in his Diaries and Correspondence. Selected by his wife, and adapted from the original German by A. D. COLERIDGE. $2.00.

" The diary and letters between them contain notices and criticisms on almost every musical celebrity of the last half-century."—*Pall Mall Gazette.*

Chorley's (H. F.) Recent Art and Society, as described in his Autobiography and Memoirs. Compiled from the edition of Henry G. Hewlett, by C. H. JONES. $2.00.

Wagner's (R.) Art Life and Theories. Selected from his Writings, and translated by EDWARD L. BURLINGAME. With a preface, a catalogue of Wagner's published works, and drawings of the Bayreuth Opera House. $2.00.

" A book which will not only be interesting to all lovers of music, but entertaining, at least in some of the chapters, to the general reader."—*N. Y. Tribune.*

Thornbury's (Walter) Life of J. M. W. Turner, R.A. Founded on Letters and Papers furnished by his friends and fellow academicians. With illustrations, fac-similed in colors, from Turner's original drawings. $2.75.

" The author has told fully and fearlessly the story of Turner's life as far as he could learn it, and has filled his pages with anecdotes which illustrate the painter's character and habits, and his book is, therefore, one of great interest."—*N. Y. Evening Post.*

Lewes (George Henry) on Actors and the Art of Acting. $1.50.

" It is valuable, first, as the record of the impressions produced upon a mind of singular sensibility by many actors of renown, and lastly, indeed chiefly, because it formulates and reiterates sound opinions upon the little-understood principles of the art of acting. . . . . Perhaps the best work in English on the actor's art."—*Nation.*

BRASSEY'S (MRS.) SUNSHINE AND STORM IN THE EAST, or Cruises to Cyprus and Constantinople. With two maps and 114 illustrations. 8vo. $3.50.

"Delightfully fresh and pleasing. . . . There is not a chapter in it from which we might not cull something that would enrich this column."—*N. Y. Eve. Post.*

"Her unpretending recital of travel and adventure has the charm as well as the simplicity of friendly talk around the domestic fireside."—*N. Y. Tribune.*

"The most lively and entertaining book we have read for many months."—*London Saturday Review.*

BRASSEY'S (MRS.) AROUND THE WORLD IN THE YACHT "SUNBEAM." Our Home on the Ocean for Eleven Months. With chart and illustrations. 8vo. $2.00.

"We close the book with a wish that, as Alexander sighed for other worlds to conquer, so there were other worlds for the 'Sunbeam' to circumnavigate."—*Literary World.*

"It is altogether unlike all other books of travel. . . . We can but faintly indicate what the reader may look for in this unrivalled book."—*London Spectator.*

GROHMAN'S (W. A. BAILLIE) GADDINGS WITH A PRIMITIVE PEOPLE. Being a Series of Sketches of Tyrolese Life and Customs. 16mo. (Leisure Hour Series.) $1.00.

"He has a bright, easy style, and, indeed, most of his adventures are so extraordinary as almost to verge on the brink of the incredible. We can recommend the book as singularly readable from the first chapter to the last."—*Saturday Review.*

BEERBOHM'S (JULIUS) WANDERINGS IN PATAGONIA, or Life Among the Ostrich Hunters. 16mo, with map and illustrations. (Leisure Hour Series.) $1.00.

"Mr. Beerbohm is a thorough master of the art of telling a story, and the simplicity and directness with which he narrates his adventures carry a conviction of truth to the reader's mind that might well excite the envy of many a hardened writer of fiction. . . . Remarkably interesting."—*Nation.*

PUMPELLY'S (R.) ACROSS AMERICA AND ASIA. Notes of a Five Years' Journey Around the World, and of Residence in Arizona, Japan, and China. With maps, woodcuts, and lithographic fac-similes of Japanese color-printing. 8vo. $2.50.

"One of the most interesting books of travel we have ever read. . . . We have great admiration of the book, and feel great respect for the author for his intelligence, humanity, manliness, and philosophic spirit, which are conspicuous throughout his writings."—*Nation.*

MORELET'S (ARTHUR) TRAVELS IN CENTRAL AMERICA. Including Accounts of some Regions Unexplored since the Conquest. Introduction and Notes by E. GEO. SQUIER. Post 8vo. Illus. $2.00.

"One of the most interesting books of travel we have read for a long time. . . . His descriptions are evidently truthful, as he seems penetrated with true scientific spirit."—*Nation.*

ESCOTT'S (T. H. S.) ENGLAND. Her People, Polity, and Pursuits. 8vo. $4.00.

"A large and exhaustive treatise on England. . . . A most useful work. . . . A massive achievement, and one which is likely to do excellent service."—*Saturday Review.*

"It is a work of real value and usefulness on England as a people and a nation, and gives information about that country which it is impossible to find elsewhere in so convenient and interesting form."—*N. Y. Tribune.*

"One of those sterling though unpretentious books whose value is permanent. . . . Rests on a philosophy so sound, and moves within information so accurate, that many generations to come will have to learn from him how England lived and felt and acted in 1880. . . . To Americans it is nothing less than a revelation. . . . The most perfect and satisfactory study in practical sociology now in existence."—*Boston Advertiser.*

WALLACE'S (D. MACKENZIE) RUSSIA. With two maps. 8vo. $4.00.

"One of the stoutest and most honest pieces of work produced in our time, and the man who has produced it, . . . even if he never does anything more, will not have lived in vain."—*Fortnightly Review.*

"Excellent and interesting. . . . worthy of the highest praise. . . . We commend his book as a very valuable account of a very interesting people."—*Nation.*

BAKER'S (JAMES) TURKEY. 8vo, with two maps. $4.00.

"His work, like Mr. Wallace's, is in many parts a revelation, as it has had no predecessor, which was so founded upon personal observation, and at the same time so full of that sort of detailed information about the habits, the customs, the character, and the life of the people who form its subject, which constitute its best possible explanation of history and of current events. . . . Invaluable to the student, profound or superficial, of Turkish affairs."—*N. Y. Evening Post.*

McCOAN'S (J. C.) EGYPT AS IT IS. With a map taken from the most recent survey. 8vo. $3 75.

"We can recommend Egypt as It Is to our readers as supplying a want which is most felt ; a detailed and a truthful and able account of the country as it is in its moral material and economical aspect."—*London Athenæum.*

CREASY'S (SIR EDWARD S.) HISTORY OF THE OTTOMAN TURKS. From the Beginning of their Empire to the Present Time. Large 12mo. $2.50.

"It presents a vivid and well-connected account of the six centuries of Turkish growth, conquest, and decline, interwoven with summary views of institutions, national characteristics, and causes of success and failure. It embodies also the results of the studies of a large number of earlier and later writers, and throughout evinces research, independence of judgment, and candor."—*Nation.*

JONES' (C. H.) AFRICA : The History of Exploration and Adventure as given in the leading authorities from Herodotus to Livingstone. With map and illustrations. 8vo. $5.00.

"A cyclopædia of African exploration, and a useful substitute in the library for the whole list of costly original works on that subject."—*Boston Advertiser.*

KEMBLE'S (FRANCES ANN) RECORDS OF A GIRLHOOD. Large 12mo. With Portrait. $2.50.

"This book is so charming, so entertaining, so stamped with the impress of a strong, remarkable, various nature, that we feel almost tormented in being treated to a view only of the youthful phases of character. Like most of the novels that we read, or don't read, this volume is the history of a young lady's entrance into life. Mrs. Kemble's young lady is a very brilliant and charming one, and our only complaint is that we part company with her too soon. . . . What we have here, however, is excellent reading. . . . She is naturally a writer; she has a style of her own which is full of those felicities of expression that indicate the literary sense."—*Nation.*

ALBEMARLE'S (GEORGE THOMAS, EARL OF) FIFTY YEARS OF MY LIFE. With a Portrait by JEENS. Large 12mo. $2.50.

"Lord Albemarle has done wisely to publish his Recollections, for there are few men who have had the opportunities of seeing so much of life and character as he has, and still fewer who at an advanced age could write an autobiography in which we have opinions without twaddle, gossip without malice, and stories not marred in the telling."—*London Academy.*

COX'S (G. W.) POPULAR ROMANCES OF THE MIDDLE AGES. By Sir GEORGE W. COX and EUSTACE HINTON JONES. Large 12mo. $2.25.

"The most important tales of the mediæval legendary lore. . . . In many cases they are found only in books that are not easily accessible, or have taken monotonous or wearisome shapes. The version now offered to the public cannot fail to be received with curiosity and interest."—*N. Y. Tribune.*

"A book of the rarest interest to all lovers of literature."—*N. Y. Eve. Post.*

"In no one English book has so rich a store of great legends ever before been collected. To praise this wonderfully delightful volume is a mere waste of words." —*Phila. Times.*

GAUTIER'S (THEOPHILE) WORKS.

A Winter in Russia. Translated by M. M. RIPLEY. 12mo. $1.75.

"As little like the ordinary book of travel as a slender antique vase filled with the perfumed wine of Horatian banquets is like the fat comfortable tea-cup of a modern breakfast-table."—*N. Y. Tribune.*

"The book is a charming one, and nothing approaching it in merit has been written on the outward face of things in Russia. . . . He sees pictures where most people find mere dead surfaces; and where common eyes find the tint of a picture, he constructs a complete work of art."—*Nation.*

Constantinople. Translated by Robert Howe Gould, M.A. 12mo. $1.75.

"It is never too late in the day to reproduce the sparkling description and acute reflections of so brilliant a master of style as the present author."—*N. Y. Tribune.*

Capitaine Fracasse. Translated by M. M. Ripley. 12mo. (*In press.*)

TAINE'S (HIPPOLYTE ADOLPHE) WORKS. Uniform Library Edition. 14 vols., large 12mo. $2.50 per vol.

> "The paper, print, and binding of this series leave nothing to be desired in point ste and attractiveness."—*Nation.*

The French Revolution. Vol. I. Translated by John Durand. Large 12mo. $2.50.

The Ancient Régime. Translated by John Durand. $2.50.

History of English Literature. Translated by H. Van Laun. 3 vols. $7.50.

On Intelligence. Translated by T. D. Haye. 2 vols. $5.00.

Italy. (Rome and Naples.) Tr. by John Durand. $2.50.

Italy. (Florence and Venice.) Tr. by John Durand. $2.50.

Notes on Paris. Tr. by John Austin Stevens. $2.50.

Notes on England. Tr. by W. F. Rae. With portrait. $2.50.

A Tour Through the Pyrenees. Tr. by J. Stafford Fiske. $2.50.

Lectures on Art. Translated by John Durand. *First Series.* (Containing the Philosophy of Art; The Ideal in Art.) $2.50.

Lectures on Art. Translated by John Durand. *Second Series.* (Containing the Philosophy of Art in Italy; The Philosophy of Art in the Netherlands; The Philosophy of Art in Greece.) $2.50.

SEPARATE EDITIONS.

A Tour through the Pyrenees. Tr. by J. Stafford Fiske. Illus. by Gustave Doré. Sq. 8vo, gilt, $10. Levant mor., $20.

> "A marvel of beauty."—*Boston Transcript.*

History of English Literature. Translated by H. Van Laun. 2 vols. 8vo, $7.50; the same in 1 vol., $4.00; the same, large 12mo, $1.25.

The Class-room Taine. History of English Literature by H. A. Taine. Abridged from the translation of H. Van Laun, and edited with chronological table, notes, and index, by John Fiske. Large 12mo. $2.00.

SYMONDS' (JOHN ADDINGTON) RENAISSANCE IN ITALY. The Fine Arts. 8vo. $3.50.

> "Much information otherwise widely scattered, and to be sought for within the covers of many books, old and new, is here put together in readable shape. The results of the late archæological research and of recent critical examinations into historical authorities and monuments of art, are here given with sufficient thoroughness. The whole book, indeed, is composed in the light of the most modern knowledge and opinion, and is quite free from the legendary story-telling tone."—*Nation.*
>
> "A most delightful book, brimful of interest and information."—*Boston Advertiser.*
>
> "A clear and symmetrical narrative in a very pleasing style."—*Atlantic Monthly.*

BOSWELL'S (J.) LIFE OF JOHNSON, including a Tour to the Hebrides. The Original Text relieved from passages of obsolete interest. $2.00.

"We do not see why this should not become the generally accepted edition of Boswell's work. . . . For those who wish to merely know Johnson and his friends, this is certainly sufficient. Nothing of that most wholesome and human presence is perceptibly lost, nor is any figure lacking in that great and charming company of which it was the centre."—*Atlantic Monthly.*

JOHNSON'S CHIEF LIVES OF THE POETS: Milton, Dryden, Swift, Addison, Pope, Gray, and Macaulay's "Life of Johnson." Selected and prefaced by Matthew Arnold, to which are appended Macaulay's and Carlyle's Essays on Boswell's "Life of Johnson." Large 12mo. $2.00.

"The compendious story of a whole important age in English literature told by a great man, and in a performance which is itself a piece of English literature of the first class. . . . I know of no such first-rate piece of literature for supplying in this way the wants of the literary student."—*Matthew Arnold.*

MARTINEAU'S (H.) BIOGRAPHICAL SKETCHES. 8vo. $1.50.

There are over fifty eminent persons "sketched" in this volume.

"Miss Martineau's large literary power, and her fine intellectual training, make these little sketches more instructive, and constitute them more generally works of art, than many more ambitious and diffuse biographies.—*Fortnightly Review.*

CHESNEY'S (C. C.) MILITARY BIOGRAPHY. Large 12mo. $2.50.

"Very able."—*Nation.*

"Full of interest, not only to the professional soldier, but to the general reader."—*Boston Globe.*

HOUGHTON'S (LORD) MONOGRAPHS, PERSONAL AND SOCIAL. With Portraits of WALTER SAVAGE LANDOR, CHARLES BULLER, HARRIET LADY ASHBURTON, and SULEIMAN PASHA. 12mo. $2.00.

"He has something new to tell of every one of his subjects. His book is a choice olio of fine fruits."—*London Saturday Review.*

SAINTE-BEUVE'S (C. A.) ENGLISH PORTRAITS. Selected and Translated from the "Causeries du Lundi." With an Introductory Chapter on Sainte-Beuve's Life and Writings. 12mo. $2.00.

CONTENTS:—Sainte-Beuve's Life—His Writings—General Comments—Mary, Queen of Scots—Lord Chesterfield—Benjamin Franklin—Edward Gibbon—William Cowper—English Literature by H. Taine—Pope as Poet.

"A charming volume, and one that may be made a companion, in the confident assurance that the better we know it, the better we shall enjoy it."—*Boston Advertiser.*

CORY'S (WILLIAM) A GUIDE TO MODERN ENGLISH HISTORY. Part I. 1815-1830. 8vo.

HISTORY OF AMERICAN POLITICS. By ALEXANDER JOHNSTON, A.M. 16mo. 75 cts.

"Clear, condensed, dispassionate. . . . His very satisfactory little volume. The design of the book is not to criticise party management, but to make the facts of our Political History easily available, and to teach our younger citizens that true, natural party differences have a history and a recognized basis of existence. The author has done his work intelligently, and with an impartiality that should invite confidence."—*Harper's Monthly.*

ADAMS' (PROF. C. K.) DEMOCRACY AND MONARCHY IN FRANCE, from the Inception of the Great Revolution to the Overthrow of the Second Empire. By Prof. C. K. Adams, of the University of Michigan. Large 12mo. Cloth, $2.50.

"A valuable example of the scientific mode of dealing with political problems." —*Nation.*

"Full of shrewd and suggestive criticism, and few readers will peruse it without gaining new ideas on the subject."—*London Saturday Review.*

"Remarkably lucid writing."—*London Academy.*

FREEMAN'S (EDWARD A.) HISTORICAL COURSE.

A series of historical works on a plan entirely different from that of any before published for the general reader or educational purposes. It embodies the results of the latest scholarship in comparative philology, mythology, and the philosophy of history. Uniform volumes. 16mo.

1. **General Sketch of History.** By EDWARD A. FREEMAN, D.C.L. 16mo. $1.40.
2. **History of England.** By Miss EDITH THOMPSON. $1.00.
3. **History of Scotland.** By MARGARET MACARTHUR. $1.00.
4. **History of Italy.** By Rev. W. HUNT, M.A. $1.00.
5. **History of Germany.** By JAMES SIME. $1.00.
6. **History of the United States.** By J. A. DOYLE. With maps by Francis A. Walker, Prof. in Yale College. $1.25.
7. **History of France.** By C. M. YONGE. $1.00.
8. **History of Greece.** By J. ANNAN BRYCE. (*In preparation.*)

"Useful not only for school study, but for the library."—*Boston Advertiser.*

STILLMAN'S (W. J.) CRETAN INSURRECTION OF 1866-7-8. By W. J. STILLMAN, late U. S. Consul in Crete. 12mo. $1.50.

"A welcome and valuable addition to the recorded history. . . . He had from the Cretan leaders information of their operations in various parts of the island, being consulted often by them as their best friend. Thus his story contains much valuable matter which cannot easily be found elsewhere."—*Nation.*

FARRAR'S (JAMES A.) PRIMITIVE MANNERS AND CUSTOMS. 12mo. $1.75.

"'The subject Mr. Farrar endeavors to illustrate is interesting, and his knowledge so extensive, that it is scarcely possible to open the volume without finding some stimulus to curiosity, and food for thought."—*London Pall Mall Gazette.*

" Will be found by most thoughtful persons a delightful book. Certainly nothing that has come within the purview of these columns for many months has afforded the reviewer such unalloyed pleasure in the reading as Mr. Farrar's volume."—*Chicago Tribune.*

RYDBERG'S (VIKTOR) MAGIC OF THE MIDDLE AGES. 12mo. $1.50.

"It is not only exceedingly interesting, but it gives a clearer and more lasting impression of the religious philosophy of the middle ages than any other work we know of."—*Literary World.*

"At once a serious polemic work, and an entertaining sketch of the strange superstitions which have prevailed in Europe. . . . A singularly able and interesting work."—*N. Y. Evening Post.*

CONWAY'S (M. D.) DEMONOLOY AND DEVIL-LORE. 2 vols. 8vo. $7.00.

"Proves himself to be a bold and original thinker. . . . His work is valuable both as a repertory of out-of-the-way information and as an essay in psychological analysis."—*Pop. Science Monthly.*

"Most exhaustive, intelligent and intellectual treatment of the subject which has ever come under our notice. . . . He is essentially a modern philosopher, and he must have learned in his journalistic career the art of making dry bones live."—*N. Y. Times.*

"Its researches present the story of every kind of goblin, imp, spectre, dragon, and thing that walketh in darkness, that has made human life piteous since it began. It is rich in curious legends and myths of the darker sort, and it is a startling proof of the halting progress of mankind, that some of the most ancient and horrible of these superstitions—as the dread of the vampire and the were-wolf—prevail at this day in certain parts of Europe."—*North American Review.*

CONWAY'S (M. D.) Sacred Anthology. 12mo. $2.00.

" He deserves our hearty thanks for the trouble he has taken in collecting these gems, and stringing them together for the use of those who have no access to the originals, and we trust that his book will arouse a more general interest in a long-neglected and even despised branch of literature, the Sacred Books of the East."—*Prof.* MAX MULLER.

BRINTON'S (D. G.) WORKS. The Myths of the New World. A Treatise on the Symbolism and Mythology of the Red Race of America. Second edition, large 12mo. $2.50. Large-paper (first) edition. $6.00.

"The philosophical spirit in which it is written is deserving of unstinted praise, and justifies the belief that in whatever Dr. Brinton may in future contribute to the literature of Comparative Mythology, he will continue to reflect credit upon himself and his country."—*N. A. Review.*

The Religious Sentiment, its Sources and Aim. A contribution to the science and philosophy of religion. Large 12mo. $2.50.

www.ingramcontent.com/pod-product-compliance
Lightning Source LLC
Chambersburg PA
CBHW020322140726
47905CB00013B/2326